HUMAN PLUS

DAVID SIMPSON

HUMAN PLUS

Cover illustration by Jennifer Simpson
Interior design and layout by Jennifer Simpson

ISBN: **1493558285**
ISBN-13: **978-1493558285**

www.post-humannovel.com

Give feedback on the book at:
posthumanmedia@gmail.com

ACKNOWLEDGMENTS

First, I want to thank my readers, and especially those on my Facebook "likes" page and those who have left positive reviews on Amazon. It's because of your enthusiasm that this series is where it is today and that I have the career that I have. Your support has made my dream of becoming a full time writer come true, but this is only the beginning. Many of you have become my closest friends over the last year, and I cannot ever thank you enough!

I'd also like to thank my beta readers, Patricia Kenworthy, Matthew Drummey, Patrick Weddell, Adam Emrick for their time, input, and talent. This book is better because of your efforts.

I'd like to thank my editor, Autumn J Conley, for her talent and her ability to bring my work up to the next level. Thank you, Autumn.

I'd like to thank Paul Hurley for being my guy to bounce story ideas off of and for helping with the quality assurance process as well.

And, as always, I'd especially like to thank my wife. She is the cover artist, the interior designer, and the most trusted story advisor that I have. She's my partner in all things and is simply the greatest wife in the universe and all other universes as well.

PART 1

If we have learned one thing from the history of invention and discovery, it is that, in the long run — and often in the short one — the most daring prophecies seem laughably conservative.

—ARTHUR C. CLARKE

UPLOAD INITIATED

WAKING UP each day was becoming increasingly difficult. I'd open my eyes with disappointment, struggle to pull my legs over the edge of the bed, crane my neck to look over my shoulder at the sleeping woman I didn't love, then stand up, walking forth into another day of slow-motion drudgery. I was in this depressed state on the day that I found out the truth: *The world is a lie.*

I perfectly remember standing on a stage in front of a crowd of nearly 200 tech reporters, as my business partner attempted—with gusto—to introduce me as though he were introducing a prophet. He actually used the words "oracle" and "visionary," though I barely paid attention. It was as if there was a soft focus in my life that day, a blur that I'd worked to cultivate. Reality had become...increasingly nauseating.

Nevertheless, I needed to endure. I wasn't suicidal. Far from it, in fact. I wanted to reach the future so badly. I could see it every time I closed my eyes, but every time I reopened them, the vision disappeared, fading away like wisps of smoke, and all that was left was the horde of meat in front of me.

Cavemen slapped their hands together in robotic applause as the introduction ended and their "prophet" crossed the stage. Even as I forced a smile and reached the podium, the soft focus continued. Behind me, the words, "Moore's Law" were projected in a stark white font, glowing on a black background.

"Everyone has been wondering who will make the next big breakthrough in computer processing. What form will it take?" I asked rhetorically. "Today, our team has made the most significant leap thus far in the acceleration of computing speed and capability," I announced, affecting the cadence of someone who was genuinely enthusiastic. "The next step for Moore's Law, the exponential increase in the speed and processing power of information technology, is the quantum chip."

The words behind me faded into an image of a silicon chip, gleaming with CGI photons and the word "Quantum" hovering above it. The assembled media applauded raucously. They'd already read the press release. Though they couldn't possibly grasp all the implications of the breakthrough, they knew that faster and more powerful technology meant better technology, and so they smacked their meaty paws together approvingly.

I kept to my script. "In the short term, quantum chip integration into existing Smartphone technology will lead to super-secure networks, making banking and online business safer. In the longer term, the quantum chip will lead to computers and tablets that can run programs that even today's supercomputers are incapable of running."

The reaction to my pronouncements was, predictably, slack-jawed. *They have eyes to see but do not see*, I thought to myself. "To put this into perspective, a quantum computing device, using only 100 photons, could solve trillions of calculations at the same time."

Again, the assembled reporters were befuddled, dumbfounded. The impressive sounding numbers that I had quoted meant nothing to them as long as their Smartphones and aug glasses might run more smoothly in the future. There was so much that they couldn't fathom.

"The consequences of such a breakthrough are innumerable, and you know our lab's policy on secrecy..." I trailed off to let the scripted joke sink in.

There was a smattering of laughter and grunts in the auditorium. They always scripted a wry joke or two to make me seem more affable for the public.

"But just to give you some idea of what we're thinking," I continued, "keep in mind that a device with such advanced hardware would be capable, at least someday, of sensing the world around it and rapidly interpreting what it senses in a way that would mimic human intelligence quite convincingly—and that is only the tip of the iceberg. Now, as is my custom at these events, I will take a few questions."

Immediately, nearly every reporter in the room jumped to their feet and began shouting questions; in such a small venue, the effect was thunderous. Mark Olson, the deputy director and our chief financial officer, had advised me on numerous occasions to "hold" such moments, realizing they made for compelling theater. In such a scenario, I was the Shamanic figure, stirring up belief amongst my audience. It was not a scenario that I enjoyed. Theater, to me, was nauseating.

My aug glasses flashed the name of the reporter I was predetermined to call on first to answer his predetermined question. The answer I was supposed to give, already meticulously written and perfectly punctuated by an English graduate student from the university, was loaded and ready to unfurl on the minuscule TelePrompTer app on my aug glasses. All I needed to do was read my lines and stick to the script, and my reputation as the world's foremost inventor and futurist would be further cemented.

I continued to hold and feigned that I was making a random choice.

But then something happened.

The feigning began to transform. Almost before I knew it, I was committed to *actually* choosing someone randomly. For a reason I couldn't explain, I *needed* to have a choice. To save myself, I needed something real, something challenging.

"How about you?" I said, purposely pointing to someone I didn't recognize, a plain-looking woman of about thirty-five.

The thunderous roar died down, and all eyes turned to the chosen woman.

She stared up at me, her eyes locking on mine. She seemed surprised and I thought she perhaps knew something was amiss. It was possible she knew that the questions were rigged and that she'd never expected to be chosen. She remained staring at me, unable to speak.

Mark's picture suddenly appeared in the top right-hand corner of my front screen. The text, "What are you doing? That's the wrong reporter!" suddenly appeared.

I narrowed my eyes, trying to will the woman to speak. I knew once she opened her mouth, there would be no turning back. I needed her to speak. I couldn't stomach the idea of answering the scripted question, which concerned why our Center continued to produce the world's most innovative breakthroughs in information technology. It was vague. Corporate. Boring. A softball. I wanted nothing to do with it.

"Okay," I said, finally acquiescing. "It seems she might be feeling a little overwhelmed," I added, smiling.

"Simon from GizBiz!" Mark shouted via text. In reality, he was standing only a few feet behind me, smiling I'm quite sure, not letting on to those assembled that something in our carefully constructed fiction had gone askew.

I turned to Simon, a twenty-something technology writer who'd masterfully achieved the look of an unemployed person living in his parents' basement. In actuality, he was one of the country's most respected tech reporters, thanks to his in-law connection to Mark.

Simon looked up at me, his expression befuddled. His eyes briefly darted up to Mark before flashing back to mine.

"Simon," I began, resignedly, "Why don't you take a crack at it?"

"Professor," Simon began, his tone begrudging, as he was clearly trying to shake off the perceived insult of not being initially chosen, "how is it that your lab continues to produce the most innovative products..."

I'd already tuned him out. He finished speaking his question, and there was the answer, overlaid over reality, waiting for me to read it for the crowd. I refused to be a ventriloquist's dummy. I removed my aug glasses and slipped them into the pocket of my pants so as not to subject myself to the inevitable panicked messages from Mark that would undoubtedly flood the screen. Keeping my hands in my pocket, I turned away from the podium and crossed the front of the stage as I considered what to say. "I wish you could all see," I began, "the future that *I* see. It's so much more marvelous than you think. It isn't just a matter of faster phones and better graphics. It isn't one that will make you more money. Money won't even exist." I briefly turned to regard Mark; though he wore a faux grin, he looked as if he were about to burst a blood vessel in his brain. "Mark doesn't like to hear me say things like that," I added.

Everyone laughed, including Mark, though I suspected his laughter took a Herculean effort to force out.

"I've *seen* the future," I continued. "I go there in my mind as often as I can every day. I don't live here in the present with all of you. I live there, in the future. When we reach it, you'll understand why. You'll understand how unbearable the present is to me—to be limited like this, to watch people die from sicknesses that we'll be able to cure twenty years from now, to watch men and women go to war and die over oil, when energy from solar and plastics built by nanobot molecular assemblers will be abundant by 2040. In the present, we have to watch starvation killing millions of people, when food will be available via download to your replicator. We muddle around blindly on this small rock in a vast ocean of wonders that await our exploration. We're trapped here like flightless birds, but we will be soaring through the cosmos just decades from now. These are the things that I cannot stand about the present." I looked up to see the audience perplexed, which was as I expected. "I prefer the future. I serve the future, and for me, it can't come soon enough."

Somewhere in the back of my mind, I imagined stock prices dropping as headlines proclaimed that the CEO of the world's most innovative technology company had gone insane. It was a brief consideration, for I had no patience for business.

I slipped my aug glasses back out of my pocket and put them back on, then smiled out at the onlookers. "Our philosophy here has always been not to look at the world as it is, but to look at it the way we want it to be, and then to make it that way. That's how we stay ahead of the competition. It's how we jettison ourselves to the future. Thank you."

And with that, I exited stage left to a standing ovation. I suddenly thought of Shakespeare. All the world was, indeed, a stage and I remained a player, despite my ardent efforts to break free.

2

I walked up the slight incline on the small avenue adjacent to the Convention Center toward the corner, knowing my car would be picking me up in less than two minutes. I kept my head down low, but as usual, dozens of passersby looked up at me, their aug glasses recognizing me and alerting them that the inventor of half of the technological gadgetry that adorned their bodies was in very close proximity. The facial recognition application, appropriately dubbed "Paparazzo," came preloaded on most aug glasses; it had turned the entire world into gawkers and stalkers. Thus, I kept my head down and charged forward, attempting to send the message to the world that I was a very busy man and should not be approached.

Meanwhile, Mark's profile picture continued flashing in my field of vision. Desperate text messages, such as "We need to talk" and "Please wait!" popped up so quickly that I suspected he had them preloaded into his aug glasses. The board of directors had insisted unanimously in a private meeting that Mark's glasses would always be linked to mine, lest their mildly autistic CEO run wild, destroying investor confidence and ruining the company with his erratic behavior. I was contractually obligated not to place him on a block list, even temporarily, and he was entitled to know my whereabouts at all times.

"I'm waiting for my car, Mark," I replied, the text appearing almost as quickly as I spoke it in a cartoon word bubble. "Better hurry. Send."

I slowed my pace as I approached the corner. I checked the GPS to see that the car was still sitting at the exit of the underground parking complex it had found nearly a kilometer away. I flipped to the dash camera and saw that it was sitting silently behind two cars at a toll booth. The hand of the driver of the front car was fumbling with a plastic card and a debit machine. I barely resisted the urge to groan as I considered the driver's obvious resistance to superior technology. *He hasn't activated a Passbook account? He drove his own car? Why? Why on Earth?* My car couldn't comprehend this caveman-like behavior and, thus, could not generate a new ETA; after all, how can one place a precise time measurement on human irrationality? It would be...infinite.

I turned back to the Convention Center and saw Mark jogging up the incline toward me. He was famous too, if far less so than I was. I wondered what UHD videos uploaded to YouTube of him jogging up the road to wrangle me would do to the stock price.

It was raining. The rain was cold—icy. An autumn wind was cutting through my light sweater, stinging my skin. I hated it, but even more so, I hated the feeling that I couldn't stop it. All I could do was hunch my shoulders slightly and keep my arms tight to my body to conserve heat, no better than a snow owl tucking its beak into its feathers. No better. *How could I be no better?* I thought. *Why am I prisoner to my physiology?* I was a prisoner to meat, just like everyone else.

"Beat your car!" Mark exclaimed, half-exasperated and half-proud of his achievement as he tried to catch his breath. "I gotta hit the gym, man."

"Or you could have conversations the way everyone else does," I replied, pointing to my aug glasses.

He bent over, propping himself up by placing his hands above his knees. "You can't beat face to face for some things," he said, shaking his head. "This is important. What the hell happened back there?"

I turned away and looked down the street in the direction from which my car would be coming. It was finally exiting the parking complex and, in sixty seconds, it would arrive. "I saved it, didn't I?"

"Yeah, you did," Mark replied, "but it was a close one. You nearly gave me a heart attack. You know you can't go off script like that."

"If my photographic memory serves, I'm still CEO," I replied, somewhat tersely.

"Yes," Mark answered, "and I want to keep it that way. Look, I'm doing everything I can to keep you inline so we can make it to the finish line together. If you go off script like that and start talking to people who aren't predetermined..."

"I get it."

"Do you? Because this isn't the first time we've had this talk."

"Oh I get it. Stick to the script. Be a prisoner to the board of my own company."

"That board meeting happened for a reason. We're all on your side. We want to see you succeed, but sometimes you're your own worst enemy."

I turned to him, my face like stone. I had nothing to say in response. *What can I say that would be worth my time?* I thought. *These are the concerns of apes.* I didn't feel the necessity to placate them with a banana.

Mark sighed. "I think it's time we revisit the idea of you talking to someone."

That got my attention. He meant a psychiatrist. I grimaced.

"It can't be easy going through life with your...illness," Mark continued.

"High-functioning autism isn't an illness," I retorted. "It's a *difference*." I said, being generous. In my view, my "condition" was a gift.

"I'm sorry. Still, it can't be easy being different, right?"

The conversation was becoming unnecessarily tangled in the sticky wetness of emotion. Psychiatrist visits were a very real threat— another part of the board's demands if I wanted to hold my position at the head of my own company. If Mark saw fit, he could force me to undergo treatment and therapy. The idea of a monkey, albeit a slightly more sophisticated than average one, probing inside of my mind as though she were looking for tiny insects to pick out and pop into her mouth disgusted me. Out of necessity, I switched my tone. I opted to confide in Mark. He was hungering for emotion, so I decided to give him a taste. "That won't be necessary," I replied, sighing as I watched my car finally appear from around the corner. The ETA flashed to eighteen seconds, and it appeared that it would arrive exactly on time. "You're right. I shouldn't have acted that way. I've been...distracted."

"What's going on?" Mark asked.

The artificial electric *buzz* of my car engine grew louder as the vehicle pulled up to the curb. The back door opened automatically upon its arrival, as if by the hand of an invisible chauffeur. "Hello, Professor," it spoke to me in a sultry, feminine voice. "Please enter."

"Would you like a lift?" I asked Mark, arching a brow.

"Yeah, sure," Mark replied. He pressed a button on his aug glasses and spoke to his own car, most likely still parked in the same parking complex where mine had been. "Go home," he ordered.

We stepped into the car together, relieved to get out of the rain. The interior of the vehicle had already warmed, and the front seats pushed forward so that Mark and I had ample leg room. "Take us to Mark's house," I said.

"Okay, Professor," the car replied. "I will take us to Mark's house."

I slipped off my aug glasses and started to put them into the front pocket of my shirt; it was a deliberate gesture to send the semiotic signal to Mark that I was fully engaged with his concerns and taking them seriously.

"Whoa, wait," Mark suddenly said, holding up his hand to stop me. "Let's have a game of chess while we talk. What do you say?"

I grinned as I finished placing the glasses into my pocket. "Sure, let's play. Set it up."

His eyes narrowed. "Are you serious? I've made you so cocky that now you're going to play me blindfolded?"

"Perhaps," I said, nodding. "Let's see if my cockiness is justified, shall we?"

"All right," Mark replied, "if you're sure." He rubbed his index finger against the arm of his glasses and then spoke, "Chess. New Game." A moment later, he craned his neck, his eyes focusing on what was an image of a chess board overlaid over his vision. The board was invisible to me, but it didn't matter. I'd long since observed that my working memory was far superior to that of normal people. While people could normally only hold about seven items of information in their short-term working memory at once, I was able to hold almost unlimited amounts of information with my photographic memory. It was true, I didn't need to see the board to defeat Mark; I'd never lost to him, though, to his credit, he'd pluckily come back for another game after every defeat; I had to respect that. However, I wasn't in the mood for a long game that day. I decided to obliterate him quickly. "I'll be white. E2 to E4."

"Okay," Mark replied. "E7 to E5," he said casually; I could tell by his tone that he had no idea what was coming. "So?" Mark asked, returning to the matter of my behavior, holding on to my nugget of revelation like a lion holding a zebra's tail between its teeth, insisting on more than a morsel.

"So..." I began with a shrug, "I'm breaking it off with Kali today."

Mark's eyes widened. "Oh."

The car rolled forward, taking us efficiently out of the downtown core, toward the bridge, and our eventual destination: Mark's beautiful mansion on the mountain that overlooked the city. The drive would last nine minutes and seven seconds in total, according to the readout that had been displayed on my aug glasses before we departed. I needed to display enough emotion to get Mark off my back by the time we arrived, convincing him that my behavior was normal considering the heartbreaking circumstances of a breakup, thus allowing me to avoid the psychiatrist land mine. Again, I would be acting. The nausea returned.

"It's just been tough," I elaborated. "She's a great person but..." I pouted my bottom lip slightly, "I'm just not happy with her. Bishop F1 to C4."

Mark's expression was grim surprise as he watched my virtual chess piece move across the board. "Are you sure you want to do it?" Mark asked. "Dump Kali, I mean. She's been a great, stabilizing influence in your life."

"Not as much as you might think," I replied and I wasn't lying. Every word I spoke was true—it was the emotion that was a lie. The truth was that I felt relief about the impending end of the relationship. Kali, my girlfriend of two years, had been an anchor, but only the kind tied around my neck, strangling me, and I was looking forward to cutting the chain.

Mark's face was still as he concentrated all of his mental power on his next move, both in the game and in life. "Knight B8 to B6. If the problem you're having is making an emotional connection with her because of your HFA, that's the exact sort of thing a psychiatrist could help you with."

It was difficult to remain patient. I hated it when people—especially Mark or Kali—used my autism as an explanation for any behavior with which they didn't agree. I knew I had to keep my temper in check, though, so I forced as convincing a smile as I could muster. "Mark, not everything can be blamed on my HFA. Some people just aren't a good match. Relationships end every day. I mean, you've been divorced twice, right?" Mark's eyes shot up to meet mine, and I made sure mine were smiling.

"Heh. Touché, I guess."

He forced a smile.

"Queen D1 to H5, by the way," I added.

"Whoa. Queen already? You're really going for the jugular here."

"I'm just being decisive," I replied, continuing to wear my smile mask.

Like a boxer rocked by a series of upper cuts in the first round, Mark tried to refocus, his eyes burning intensely into the invisible board. "Uh...Knight G8 to F6. I think. Wait. Damn it."

He'd walked right into my trap. "Queen H5 to F7. Check mate."

Mark scratched his head. "That was quick."

"I apologize," I offered. "It's a short car ride and I wanted you to see that my faculties are as sharp as ever." I leaned in and smiled, reassuringly. "I'm going to be okay, my friend."

"I really hope so," Mark replied as he tried to shake off the shock of defeat. He turned and watched the city recede into the heavy, gray cloud cover behind us as we crossed the bridge. "I really do. I've invested a lot of time in you. I'm rooting for you, buddy. I want you to succeed in everything."

My poker face melted, and my brow furrowed for an instant as I considered his strange and unexpected emotional effusion. "Uh...I appreciate that, Mark," I quickly replied, reestablishing my smile.

"I'm being serious," Mark said, leaning in closer, his eyes dripping with earnestness. "I've spent the last two years watching you because I believe in you. I know you don't like it. I know you think of me like a pesky glorified babysitter. But you have to understand, I don't enjoy it either. I watch over you because I want to see you get where you're supposed to go."

"I'm sorry, Mark. I didn't know you felt that way," I said sincerely. "I guess I hadn't considered how taxing it must be for you."

He smiled and shook his head. "You have no idea."

Mark's house appeared from out of the gray nothingness, as though it had just been imagined by God. My car rolled to a stop outside of the large, black gate. Mark grinned and patted my leg reassuringly, then stepped out of the vehicle.

He turned back to the car and leaned down to the window, his earnest expression returning. "For all your genius, you really have no idea how important you are," he said. "The whole company is depending on you." He smiled again. "Heck, when you really think about it, the whole world is depending on you."

"Drop me off at the front entrance," I told the car as we neared my building.

"Okay. I will drop you off at the front entrance. Shall I park myself in the underground garage?"

"Yes."

"Okay. I will park myself in the underground garage."

The door opened the moment the car came to a full stop and I stepped out immediately. I slipped my aug glasses back on.

"Goodbye, Professor."

The door of the car closed behind me as the front door of my building opened, triggered by the location software in my aug glasses. "Where's Kali?" I asked.

"Kali is home," my glasses responded as the elevator door slid open to allow for my entrance before efficiently closing behind me. The light for the PH button illuminated automatically as I leaned against the chrome railing that ran along the mirrored walls of the elevator. I briefly considered my image in multiplicity, one reflection echoing infinitely and I was reminded of a Hall of Mirrors.

When the door opened to my penthouse apartment, Kali was waiting for me, her eyes bright and beautiful, though unable to hold my attention. My gaze immediately dropped—automatically, primally—to devour the tan, moisturized skin on abundant display. She was wearing a peekaboo nightie that revealed her enticing red lace bra and matching panties that barely covered her remarkable assets. She was making things difficult.

"Surprise!" she exclaimed as she threw her arms around my shoulders.

"I'm surprised," I replied. "What's the occasion?"

"We're celebrating your keynote, obviously!" she announced, rolling her eyes and shaking her head as she grabbed my hand and pulled me into our shared apartment. Only a few paces to the left, she'd left an open bottle of champagne to chill in a bucket of ice and two glasses were already filled and waiting. She sat me on the barstool and deftly grasped both flutes, then handed me one and placed a warm, delicious kiss on my mouth. It was a long kiss, and there was something behind it that pulled me in like gravity—there was purpose behind it—strategy. When she finally pulled her lips away from mine, her eyes were earnest and close. She sipped the champagne, her other hand over my shoulder, gently on my back. "We're gonna have a great night tonight, okay? Just you and me. What do you say?"

Freud's *Civilization and its Discontents* screamed in my ears. This was it—I'd reached it. This was the moment when I had to give my reason precedence over my bodily urges. I can't lie: it was not easy. Kali was as gorgeous a woman as I had ever seen in my life. Her hair was jet black, her skin brown and smooth, and her eyes adorned with flecks of jade that seemed to light up like an LED screen. However, even those attributes weren't the most irresistible, the most desirable. Her curves—they were absolute perfection. She had a sway in her hips and breasts that only men (and the very few women who have it) understand for its intoxicating power. She made women that could have been lingerie models cry themselves to sleep in envy.

Still, there I was, trying to break it off with *her*...for science.

She seemed to be able to sense the conflict churning inside me, even if she had no idea how serious it was or how close she was to coming out on the losing end. The corner of her lip curled into a mischievous grin. "Oh no. There's no way you're gonna blow me off for work, gorgeous." She stepped back and flicked the delicate spaghetti strap off one of her shoulders, allowing her bra to drop dangerously close to revealing a nipple.

I stood immediately, convinced that the appearance of a fully exposed breast would spell the end of my ability to put mind over matter. "Kali, no. I...can't. We have to talk."

"Talk is boring," she purred. "So much more can be accomplished without words," she teased, still smiling as she stepped closer and brushed her smooth skin against mine.

"I'm serious, Kali."

She stepped back half a step and wrinkled her brow. "What is it?"

I stepped back myself, putting more distance between myself and her temptation. "I want to end our relationship," I finally said, bluntly. I instantly felt relieved.

The smile on Kali's face melted in an instant. Her eyes seemed to glaze over, tracking me one minute, the next sitting fixed and deadened. There was no disbelief, no hope, no assumption that I could possibly be joking. She simply looked...vacant.

"Kali?" I asked after several moments of silence. "Kali. I know this is hard, but you have to say something."

She remained perfectly still and said nothing.

I sighed, turned, and sat on the barstool again. I suddenly felt the urge to escape reality, to get out of my head. I wasn't one to drink, but I knocked back the entire glass of champagne in a few gulps. When I finished, I set the stemware back on the counter, then turned back to Kali, who hadn't moved—not even in the slightest. A chill tickled over my skin as I watched the uncanny display; it felt as though the life had left her body, yet her corpse remained upright, eyes open, face like an emotionless mask. I slowly stood to my feet and walked toward her, my eyes fixed on hers, scanning for even the slightest movement or sign of life. "Kali?" I asked again. I was suddenly terrified. *Did she just have a psychotic break right in front of my eyes?* I wondered. I had no idea that she'd react that way. I continued to step slowly toward her, crouching low to try to get my face directly into her line of sight, hoping I could get her eyes to start tracking mine again, at the very least. There remained no sign of consciousness, though her chest continued to slowly expand and contract as she breathed. I waved my hand in front of her eyes.

Finally, she shook her head violently, as though waking from a bad dream. She looked at me, aghast, and then turned her head to take in the apartment, as though she'd just arrived.

Unconsciously, my eyes flashed down to take in the primal pleasure of skin that was still on display.

The gesture wasn't lost on her, and she looked down at herself, her face suddenly contorting, as though she were repulsed and ashamed of her own body. "Oh my God," she whispered. She hurried across the room to the coatrack and wrapped herself in the longest one, pulling it over herself and tightening the belt. When she was done, clothing herself, she looked up at me with a confused, but also ashamed expression that baffled me; I could have sworn I was in the presence of a completely different person from the woman who'd greeted me at the elevator door minutes earlier in nothing but her skivvies and a ridiculously impractical negligee.

"So...what are you talking about? What's going on?" she asked, as though she were more interested in getting my focus off of her body than onto our breakup. I had placed something ahead of her body on my list of priorities, and coming to terms with the realization was apparently not easy for her. It was as if she'd been rebooted right before my eyes.

"I'm sorry, Kali, but I want to end our relationship. It's time for us to go our separate ways."

Kali stood still, her arms crossed in front of her body as she stared at me again. This time, though, it was clear that she understood; I could see her thoughts racing behind her eyes as she considered her next move. "Can we..." she began to say before quickly abandoning the request.

I shrugged. "I'm sorry. I have to do this."

"But why?"

"My work. My work is what makes me what I am. It's everything to me—to everyone. My work is more important than me, than my competitors—it's more important that even a romantic relationship. My work gives my life meaning, Kali. It justifies my existence."

Kali's face twitched slightly, but again she was silent. Still, slight movements of her eyes assured me she was fully engaged, still contemplating her next move. She was no longer in shock. "You can be so damn insufferable," she said, shaking her head. "Do you *ever* have your own unique thoughts? Or is everything you say recited straight out of a book?"

Her words terrified me. It didn't bother me that they were hostile or derisive. What terrified me was that she was right—but she shouldn't have been. *How in the world could she possibly know?* I asked myself. I bet that she was bluffing. "I don't know what you're talking—"

"Yes you do," she responded sharply. "You're paraphrasing Freud. And I quote, 'No other technique for the conduct of life attaches the individual so firmly to reality as laying emphasis on work; for his work at least gives him a secure place in a portion of reality, in the human community. The possibility it offers of displacing a large amount of libidinal components, whether narcissistic, aggressive or even erotic, on to professional work and on to the human relations connected with it lends it a value by no means second to what it enjoys as something indispensable to the preservation and justification of existence in society.' End quote."

My lips parted but my astonishment dumbfounded me. She'd just quoted Freud's *Civilization and its Discontents* verbatim. It was true that I'd paraphrased it, as it had informed much of my thinking in the previous weeks while I considered ending my relationship, but I didn't know how she could possibly know that. She wasn't wearing aug glasses, and even if she had been, the paraphrase was so loose that it couldn't have triggered any plagiarism detection software. While I had a photographic memory and an IQ that rendered traditional intelligence testing useless, Kali was just a normal, slightly above average intelligence human being—or at least I'd always assumed so. "How...?" I muttered.

"You've really annoyed me today, you know that? Do you even care?" she said, her mouth pulled into a grimace as she ignored my query, her arms remaining folded tightly across her chest. "You're the most difficult puzzle I've ever had to solve."

"I..." I couldn't speak. For the first time I could remember, I was completely stymied.

Kali dropped her arms and sighed, looking around the spacious, luxurious interior of our apartment, her eyes finally settling on the dark, rainy day outside. "Two years. This was the farthest I've made it so far. I don't want to have to start over again."

"Kali," I began, my tone soft, "how did you—"

"You know how I did it," she asserted, snapping her head around to lock her stern eyes on mine. "You may be the only one of your kind with the ability to figure it out, but you *can* figure it out—not that it'll do you any good."

For the second time, her words terrified me. Indeed, a possible explanation *had* occurred to me, but it seemed so outlandish that I couldn't bring myself to believe it.

She didn't seem interested in filling me in. Rather, she focused on herself. "Tell me what I did wrong," she suddenly demanded, stepping toward me, her eyes earnest and determined. "Help me understand what it is you want so that this doesn't happen again."

I felt helpless, as if the whole world was a bucking bronco that had shaken me off. "Kali..." I began to stammer. "I don't think that's a worthwhile exercise—"

"I don't care what you think. Answer the question," she demanded, this time in a tone that, considering the context, seemed absurdly threatening.

Suddenly annoyed, I made a vain effort to regain control over the confrontation by giving her exactly what she wanted. "Fine. I'll tell you. You take up far too much of my time. I want to devote my life fully to my inventions. The only reason I can possibly conceive of for staying would be if you offered me a truly loving and emotional respite so my time spent with you would be recuperative."

"A respite? Really! What are you talking about?" she reacted, exasperated as she opened her coat to reveal her nightie again. "What do you think *this* is for?"

"*That* is not recuperative," I replied. "It is exhausting. You're a gorgeous woman, Kali, but you act like a porn star when we're alone together. You're a completely different person in the bedroom. You don't even seem to know me, and you never take no for an answer."

Kali stood, stunned. "Wow. So you're telling me that I found the one man in the universe who complains that his woman wants to give him amazing sex."

This time, Raymond Chandler's wisdom emerged foremost in my mind: *It's so hard for women—even nice women—to realize that their bodies are not irresistible.* I dared not say it.

"Okay," she said, when she realized I had no answer, nodding as she crossed her arms in front of her chest again. "What else?"

"You're bizarrely controlling," I said as I nodded toward an ugly, antique china cabinet that didn't match any of our other furniture. "You won't even let me touch the damn thing...in my own home!"

"It's an antique," she replied coolly, "and I don't want you to damage it. Is it really that difficult to respect my wishes on something so trivial?"

"Actually, yes," I replied, stepping toward the cabinet, my hand outstretched, reaching for the dark wood. My plan was to leave a nice, big hand print on the surface to show her that such a transgression would not cause the world to crumble to its instant end.

Little did I know.

"No!" Kali shrieked as she reached out for me, sending an invisible force toward me—a force so powerful that it took my feet out from underneath me and slammed me against the wall with enough power to turn the whole world black.

4

"WAKE UP," Kali commanded. "I'm not through with you yet."

I was considerably dazed, a sensation completely foreign to me; it felt as though something had reached into my skull and plunged its fingers deep into the gray matter. In the wake of such a traumatic seizure, I couldn't be sure of what was real and what was not. What I thought certainly couldn't be real was that Kali had grasped the back of my shirt collar and begun to drag me with one hand across our slate gray marble floor. It occurred to me that she was, quite literally and quite absurdly, mopping the floor with me. A moment later, she thrust me back onto my barstool. A moment after that, she slapped me hard across the face. After the slap, the haze was instantly gone.

"I want you to give me a detailed list of every trait you want me to have. I want to know exactly what you want me to be like," she said, as though it were an order. "What is your perfect woman? I want to know so we can avoid this in the future."

"How-how...how did you—"

"Oh, stop it," Kali replied, cutting me off as she impatiently shook her head. "You already *know* how I did it. What you should be worried about it is making sure that I don't do it again."

"I-I really have no idea." I looked at the china cabinet. *Was it booby-trapped?* I asked myself as a series of other questions flooded my mind. Had I been hit with some sort of a taser? Had it scrambled my brain enough to make me hallucinate the rest? These explanations were desperate attempts to put my world back together, but it was a world that could never be the same again.

"The answer is so painfully obvious," Kali replied. "You already know it. You talked about it today at your keynote."

There *was* an answer that wouldn't leave my brain, like an incorrect answer that won't move aside and blocks your thinking as you struggle to conjure the correct answer on an exam. I kept pushing it aside. *It can't be right. It can't.*

Kali finally relaxed her shoulders, letting her threatening posture melt away. "You won't even dare say it, will you?" She shook her head, and I almost sensed pity—almost. "You told the whole world today that you 'live in the future.' Don't you remember?" She grinned slightly. "You thought you were being metaphorical—perhaps even poetic. What you didn't realize was that you were being literal."

"It can't be," I whispered.

"Oh, it can, and it is," she replied. "The future you described today already exists—a future without disease, without money, without poverty. It's almost indescribably beautiful. It's where *I* live." She placed her hand gently under my chin and raised my disbelieving eyes to hers. "It's where I'd like to live with you someday."

For the first time in my life, I couldn't close my agape mouth. I felt frozen.

"Do tell me you understand what I'm talking about," she said.

"I understand," I answered flatly, "but I don't believe it."

She turned away, grunting in frustration. "And why not? You theorized about this exact possibility!"

I snapped my head toward her. "What?"

"Oh, did I forget to tell you?" she began, suddenly in the mood to mock me, "I have access to all of your files. I've read everything."

I stood upright, rigid and furious. "Those files are private! The information is extraordinarily sensitive! If our investors found out—"

She threw her head back, and a shrill laughter erupted from her so quickly that she nearly spasmed. It took her a moment to regain her composure.

Again, I was left dumbfounded.

"You're worried about your investors? Darling, you have much more dire things to worry about now."

I shook my head. *It has to be a trick*, I thought to myself. For her to have infiltrated my files—it was almost unimaginable. Even with direct access to my computer, the protection software was so utterly advanced, so ridiculously next-generation, that it should have been impossible to crack—I should know—I wrote it. My thoughts were suddenly filled with suspects, people who had the resources necessary and the lack of scruples required to have masterminded such a plot—to have found a woman like Kali, who had infiltrated my life and had been performing the most sophisticated industrial espionage I could ever imagine. Kali had been in my life for two years. We lived together. We slept in the same bed every night unless I was away on business. *How much were they paying her to hack my computers?* I asked myself. To sleep with me? To taser me? A thought suddenly occurred to me and I turned to the empty champagne glass. Had she drugged me too?

She saw my eye line and chuckled. "Don't be idiotic. I didn't drug you."

"Who are you working for?" I demanded.

"I said, don't be idiotic. It's unbecoming."

I stormed toward her and reached out to grab hold of her forearm. I don't know what I was thinking; I suppose I was in denial. I was desperate to form an explanation founded in the real world. If that world were real, then the taser and drugged champagne were obstacles I could overcome, and ultimately, I could still physically dominate a woman. Unfortunately for me, the real explanation had very little to do with the real world.

As soon as my hand grasped her arm, she yanked it away before winding up and slapping me harder than I'd ever been hit in my life. An instant later, my body collided against the side of the bar, and I slumped with a wheeze to the ground, desperately trying to recapture my breath.

"Let's stop pussyfooting around the issue, shall we?" Kali announced, not even bothering to check to see if I were okay. "You wrote about this scenario yourself. You took your mathematical models for predicting the future of technological progress to their logical conclusions and dreamed up a future that would be possible within your lifetime. You remember that, don't you?"

I wiped blood from my lip and nodded. Indeed, inspired by Einstein's tendency to do daily mental exercises—exercises that led to his realization that nothing could move faster than light—I too, did my own daily mental exercises. One such exercise was to postulate what would be possible with technology that was only thirty years more advanced than our own. The conclusions were fantastic, if not also alarming.

"According to Moore's Law," Kali continued, "which has held or been exceeded in the future, you'll be glad to know, a computer's processing power doubles annually. Thirty doublings leaves you with processing power more than one billion times as powerful as current technology. You speculated that, with processing power of that magnitude, entire virtual worlds could be constructed—worlds indistinguishable from reality." She held her hands up and looked around the room. "Looks pretty real, doesn't it?"

I still couldn't believe it. I pushed myself up into a sitting position, propping my back against the bar, the toppled barstool supporting my elbow.

"But, ever the overachiever, you went further than just speculating about a super virtual world that would kick *Second Life*'s virtual ass. You, darling, made a connection that was revolutionary. You connected the expected mental enhancements of humans and the eventual transition from organic to machine brains to the creation of these virtual worlds. You speculated that, with enough enhancement, people would eventually be able to create these worlds in their own minds. You speculated that daydreams could become as real as the real world."

She was right: I'd written about it feverishly on the night I'd first conceived of it. It didn't make her story any easier for me to accept.

"Then, you went even further. You speculated that the characters in these virtual dream worlds could be created or *re-created* so accurately—not just on their surface, but also in their cognitive abilities, that they could pass the Turing test—that they could become *conscious* entities."

I was terrified. I knew where this was leading. The logic of her assertions—of what I had previously thought was only my speculations about fantastic future possibilities—was flawless. It *was* possible. Not only that—it was inevitable.

"Professor," Kali continued, leaning down to speak to me as if I were a frightened child, which I suppose I was, at least from her perspective. "You *really are* living in the future. The only problem is," she said, tapping her temple, "you're just a character in *my* daydream...and now you've gone and made me want to wake up."

5

"WAKE UP?" I reacted, gripped by a mixture of confusion and terror. "What are you saying?"

"I'm saying I'm going to have to start over." She sighed and shook her head, frustrated. "I've failed again. Just another failed experiment on my way to discovering the key."

"Failed what? What key? What are you talking about?" I leaned forward and tried to get to my feet but my chest was still burning from the blow, and my legs weren't ready to hold me up just yet.

"I've failed to make you love me," she replied, her eyes turned back to mine, appearing earnest.

"I-I don't understand this. I—"

"You understand," she interrupted. "You just don't *believe*. There's a big difference between understanding and belief. Would you like some proof?"

I wasn't sure how to respond. Did proof mean she intended to do something horrible to me? I tried to respond, but the conflict in my thought process kept me from settling on an answer. Not fond of the idea of signing my own death warrant, I kept quiet.

"Here's a quick and easy one," she replied, not waiting for my response. "Honey, what color do you think we should pick for our apartment?" She stared straight at me as the walls began to fluctuate through a rainbow of colors.

The walls had been a slate gray, matching our floor, but every half-second, they switched to a new shade. Absurdly, as they rolled through the myriad of hues, I found myself thinking that the scarlet looked particularly sharp. Nevertheless, I kept my lips sealed.

"Of course that didn't convince you," Kali correctly guessed. "You need something a little more dramatic, don't you? Not just some illusion that a hack in Vegas could pull off. You need to see real magic."

My lips remained sealed, but my eyes told a different story, one Kali easily read: I hungered for proof. I *needed* proof.

"Follow me," she said, motioning for me to follow her with her index finger before striding to our balcony. The view from our condo was of the downtown core across the bay. As on most days, it was a concrete and glass metropolis, shrouded in dark gray clouds, and the steady beat of billions of raindrops impacting in a staccato. "Ever wonder why it rains almost every day in our fair city?" she asked as the fresh sea air filled my lungs and mussed my hair. "It's because I'm only happy when it rains. For you, however, I'll make an exception."

In only seconds, the cloud cover dispersed, opening into a crystal-blue sky, backdropped by an orb so yellow and bright that I had to shield my eyes and turn away, tearing up immediately.

"Let's see Houdini pull that one off," she said.

My mouth was ajar once again. It occurred to me that I'd never seen the sun so bright or the sky so blue. I'd never seen the bay sparkle so brightly, almost like a second sun, nor the mountains lit up with such an emerald green. "It-it can't be."

"Sure it can," Kali replied. "I'm God." She snapped her fingers, and the clouds came back, rushing in from all directions, stamping out the sunshine and the blue and replacing them with the same dull, dark, gothic sky to which I'd grown so accustomed. "But as I said, I'm only happy when it rains."

Shaking, I backpedalled into the apartment. For some reason, I thought of running, as though if I made it to the elevator and escaped the apartment before this monster caught me, it might make a difference. It wouldn't, however. I was trapped. There was no escaping God.

"Convinced?" she asked.

I nodded.

"Good. Now, I need to know what you want in a perfect woman. I'm tired of failing. This is a puzzle I must solve."

"I-I don't really know," I replied, my lips quivering as I tried not to fall flat on the floor. I suddenly had the feeling that I didn't have a body—as though my arms and legs were just an illusion, like I was a floating consciousness on a sea of empty space. It was terrifying.

"You have a real opportunity here," she told me. "You can save the life of your next iteration. You can make sure *he* doesn't make the same mistake you and your predecessors have."

"What? What are you talking about?" I asked.

"I have to start over," she replied, holding up her hands, as though her statement were obvious. "I can't stay here, can I? The whole point of this world is to win your heart. If I fail, it's game over, and I have to play again."

"Kali. Seriously. What the hell?"

She tilted her head to the side, again hinting at some level of sympathy for my situation. "This is *my* dream. I want you, Professor. I want you to love me. I've wanted it for so long." She grabbed me by the arm, just as I'd tried to grab her earlier. She guided me back to my barstool and sat me down like a mother pulling her stubborn son to the corner. "Would you like another glass of champagne?" she offered in an unsettlingly casual tone. "It'll be your last."

My heart beat with the rhythm of pure horror. I nodded because I believed her. I believed everything she told me. She'd left me no alternative.

She poured the glass and handed it to me.

I found myself suddenly focusing on the fizz of the carbonation. *So many details*—it was a remarkable simulation in which I found myself. *Simply remarkable.*

"So now you understand," Kali said, her voice breathy, "and you understand the self-sacrifice you could make," she continued, handing me my last glass of champagne.

I closed my eyes and put the glass to my lips. I took in every sensation; the rim of the glass, cold against my lips, and the tingle of the carbonation as it filled my mouth and tickled my throat. Every sensation was suddenly more important than anything that had ever occurred in my life. I wanted to drink up every breath, every taste, every sensory perception that suddenly seemed to bombard me in that moment. Indeed, nothing makes you more aware of the senses life offers than your impending death.

"I want this to be the last world I have to shut down," she said. "*You* can help me, Professor. *You* can save your next iteration's life."

I believed her. In that moment, I believed in God. I had to. I'd seen enough. It was possible that I'd been drugged, that I'd hallucinated the sky change and her power to knock me senseless at will, but I knew it would be suicide to resist her game. I'd play. I'd play.

"Don't shut this world down, Kali," I said, calmly but earnestly. "This iteration isn't over—not just yet."

Kali tilted her head again, her demeanor surprised and questioning.

"I'm *alive,* Kali. If you end this world, you'll kill me. You'll have murdered me."

Her mouth formed a half-smile. "Alive? I'm sorry, darling, but from my perspective, you're really nothing at this point but potential. Your consciousness, in its current form, is worthless. You're a mosquito."

Again, her logic was flawless. It was true. To a sufficiently advanced consciousness, a human intellect, no matter how advanced it was in relation to its peers, would be nothing in comparison. For her, turning off my world was as easy a decision as the decision made by multitudes of pimply teenagers closing their latest edition of *HALO* or *Black OPS*. Why should she care? We were nothing, and our world was a fabrication that could be restarted at her will.

"Kali, I'm sorry," I said desperately. "You're right. I'm nothing. I understand that now. My next iteration will be nothing either. But the one thing I value above all else is intellect, and I understand now that yours far outweighs mine."

Her face suddenly became stone. Everything in her countenance funneled through her eyes, which locked perfectly on mine and shone with the beauty of self-idealized fiction, urging me to continue my flattery.

"You've solved your puzzle. Your failure in past simulations was that you weren't honest with me. This time, you told me the truth. You admitted your brilliance. That's always been my Achilles' heel. I had no idea what you were before. Now I know. How could I reject your love? How could I reject the love of a goddess—the one true Goddess?"

There was a moment of silence. Then her chest heaved with a sigh that told me she'd been waiting, breathlessly, for that success for a long, long time. She wrapped her arms around me and placed her cheek against mine.

"I've wanted this so badly," she admitted. "I failed in the real world, and I've failed a half a dozen times since in the virtual world, but I've finally found the key to your heart." She rocked me in her arms. "I should've known that the key to a genius's heart would be through his intellect."

The only thing that mattered to me at that moment was survival. I would've said anything to keep her virtual dream in motion. My life would continue, and that was all that mattered. She pulled back and looked deeply into my eyes. "*Now*, we should celebrate. This is an important day." I smiled up at her, doing everything I could to affect true joy, while pure terror gripped my heart.

"Let's go to the bedroom," she said, suddenly returning to the form I'd seen her in so many times previously. Domineering. Unstoppable. She grabbed hold of my hand and pulled me across the room, toward the bedroom. She pushed me into the darkness. "Strip," she insisted, her mouth open in a Cheshire Cat grin, wolfish and evil, as she slipped off her coat.

I smiled. I removed my shirt. My legs were shaking from fear.

I smiled.

6

I watched Kali, the city lights conjuring a soft glow on her skin. I marveled that God could sleep.

I, on the other hand, hadn't slept at all. I'd performed. Like an automaton, I'd smiled, kissed, caressed, and even soothed. It wasn't difficult to pretend that I was okay with all of it; when life is on the line, one inevitably finds a way.

Now that she was asleep however, all I wanted was escape. I slipped out of our bed as carefully as possible and grabbed my clothes, not daring to put them on yet, keeping a watchful eye on her the entire time as I backed into the hallway and then ran to the elevator. I slipped on my clothes as the elevator made its way up to the penthouse, and I put my aug glasses back on so the car could detect my location and pick me up out front. As the elevator doors closed behind me, my relief was overwhelming. I doubled over and began shaking, allowing the pent-up terror the release it had so desperately sought for hours.

The car was ready as I bustled out of the building and into the dark, wet night. I found myself looking at everything, at every blade of grass, at every drop of rain as it hit the pavement, astounded that I had Kali to thank for all of it. Even the air that filled my lungs came from her mind—her majestic, horrific mind.

"Hello, Professor," the car said, greeting me with a calm that I suddenly cherished. "Where would you like to go?"

"Waves Coffee Shop," I said quietly in reply, naming the only public place that I knew to be open at that time of night.

"Okay. Waves Coffee Shop it is."

As the car rolled forward, I shut my eyes, blocking Kali's world from my view. I wanted, desperately, for it all to have been a sick joke. I wanted to be the victim of the most elaborate corporate espionage in history; I wanted the mafia to be in on it; I wanted it to go to the highest levels of international government. I'd take any of those scenarios over the one I faced now—I'd take any of them over the truth.

"Here you go. We've arrived at Waves Coffee Shop," the car told me, pulling me out of my worried trance as the car door opened, letting the wet air waft in.

I opened my eyes and looked up at the neon sign. I stepped out of the car in a daze, marveled at the detail of the shop as it glowed, brilliant like Hopper's *Nighthawks* painting in the otherwise dark street.

I stepped inside, and the fresh sea air was replaced by the familiar, earthy odor of coffee and sugary baked goods. I stepped into the shop for what had to be the thousandth time in my life, yet it felt like I were traversing the surface of an as-of-yet undiscovered planet for the first time. My visage appeared, wobbled and faded, in the glass case behind which were housed cookies, cakes, donuts and sandwiches. Suddenly transfixed by the image, I leaned in, trying to get a clear view of my eyes to make sure that they were still there, desperate for evidence that I was real.

"I bet I know what you want," the young woman behind the counter said pleasantly.

My back suddenly stiffened, and I jolted upright.

"Chocolate cake, right?" she suggested with a smile. "Warm?"

I couldn't reply. Again, I found myself dumbfounded as I studied her face. The same, young, dark-haired woman with the dark brown eyes had helped me hundreds of times. I'd smiled at her so many, many times: smiles that I didn't mean; smiles that she'd returned, likely with even less meaning. However, I'd never *seen* her before— never really seen her. I'm not sure I would've even noticed her if I'd seen her on the street some afternoon. Yet in the wake of Kali's revelation to me, after my rude awakening, I couldn't get enough of the details. Every freckle, every pore on her skin, the pliability of the soft, youthful skin on her cheeks as she moved her lips to speak: I was transfixed.

"Uh...are you okay?" she asked me.

My eyes suddenly widened. I remembered that the rest of the world didn't know what I knew—I had to continue playing my part. "Sorry. Um, thank you, no. Not tonight. A London Fog. That's what I'd like. Large, please."

She nodded and smiled, though her eyes told me she'd instantly formed the opinion that I either had a mental illness or was having a difficult time coming off prescription medication.

I paid for my drink and watched her walk to the drink station to begin making my London Fog. I thought of all the interactions I'd had with her over the last few years. Had there been anything odd about them, I wondered? Had they always been simply routine? Was she an automaton? Was she just a simple construct, placed into Kali's virtual dream to serve me drinks twice a week? Or was there more to her? Was she conscious like I was? Was she truly human? Was anyone? Am I? *"Cogito, ergo sum,"* I whispered to myself.

"Pardon me?" the young woman said as she handed me my drink.

"Oh, uh...it's Latin. It means, 'I think, therefore I am.'"

Her eyes narrowed. "Right. Makes sense." She shrugged and smiled. "Me too, I guess."

I nodded. "Thank you," I said, holding up my drink and turning away from her, returning back to my daze and walking in my trance to an open table, sitting and staring forward with my warm drink in hand.

"Hey, Professor," said another young woman, this one with purple, spiky hair and more piercings on her lips, eyebrows, nose, and ears than I'd ever seen on a person in the flesh. "You need to keep up appearances. You're starting to freak people out."

"I-I'm sorry. Do I know you?" I asked as she sat down across from me, a mischievous, knowing smile painted across her black lip-sticked lips.

"I know *you*. That's what's important."

For the second time that night, my mouth hung open. "Wh-what?"

"I also know what happened to you tonight," she continued. She reached across the table and took the London Fog from my slack grip and put the cup to her lips. "Mmm. Yummy."

"Help yourself," I whispered in shock.

"You found out something tonight that messed with you pretty good, didn't you?" she said, pointing to her forehead and making a circular motion with her index finger in a clear reference to my current state of mind.

I stayed quiet, paralyzed with fear.

The girl with the purple hair leaned forward, grinning, the whites of her eyes brilliant against the black outline of her heavy eyeliner. "You're living inside someone else's head, Professor," she whispered eerily.

I couldn't breathe.

"And," she said, leaning back into her seat and propping her brown leather boots on my knee, "I bet you're just dying to get some answers."

7

"Who are you?" I whispered, my throat dry.

"The name's Haywire." She leaned forward and extended her hand to shake mine. "Nice to meet you."

"Likewise," I barely managed to say. I had no idea what the hell was going on, nor did I know who or what that woman was. I swiveled my head, scanning for exits.

Haywire laughed. "You're worried that I'm one of Kali's creations, aren't you?"

My eyes locked back on hers instantly; she seemed to know everything. It didn't make sense. *How could she possibly know?* I asked myself. The only explanation was that she was some sort of manifestation of Kali's imagination. I'd left Kali dreaming upstairs in our bedroom. Was it possible that I was caught in a dream within a dream?

"I'm not a spy. Don't worry," Haywire stated, her lips forming a sideways smirk. "However, I can't be completely sure that *you're* not, unwittingly spying on *me for her.*" She reached into her small, black purse and pulled out her phone. "So I hope you don't mind if I check. Hold still." Then she held it out in front of me, waving it over me as though she were airport security and this was her wand. The phone made a happy whistle and she smiled. "All clean. Awesome," she said as she placed her phone back into her bag. "You'll be happy to know that she hasn't bugged you."

"Bugged me?"

"Yeah, you know...with spyware." She leaned in again and whispered, "Anyone you meet could be a spy. She can see through their eyes."

I turned my head slightly and noted that the dark eyed girl behind the counter was watching us out of the corner of her eye. As soon as our eyes made contact, mine jumped back to Haywire, whose sideways smirk returned.

"Don't worry," she said. "Scanned her when I came in."

"With your phone?" I asked. "What kind of technology is—"

"Oh, it doesn't matter." She held up my London Fog and waved it over me in the same fashion as she had her phone. "*Beep, beep, beep,*" she said, each word aggravatingly high-pitched. "*Ding!* You're cleared again! Congratulations!" She took another sip of what was formerly my drink. "I can use any physical object to scan you in this simulation. The phone or the cup—they just represent the scan, just like this body you see me in just represents me—but it's *not* me. You dig? I'm just wearing it, like a skin suit."

The plot, as they say, was thickening quickly.

"It's...it's an avatar?"

"Bingo," she said, her eyes smiling at me over the lip of the stolen cup as she continued to drink.

"So...so you're not—"

"From around here? Nope. I'm from the real world, handsome."

Strange as it may sound, what stunned me most wasn't the fact that the woman had just told me she was from the real world; it was that she'd used the word "handsome" to describe me, which no one had ever done before. That my hand bolted up to touch my own cheek gave me away; I could see it in her eyes. She was flirting. Absurdly, she grinned and batted her eyes.

"The real world? You mean, you're from *Kali's* world? You're like her?"

"In the sense that I'm from her time and exist outside of this simulation, yes, I'm like her," she said, quickly adding in a slow, emphatic tone, "but I'm *not* like her in any other sense. We're worlds apart."

"What do you mean?"

"For one thing, I don't create conscious beings with my imagination to amuse myself, only to murder them when I lose interest."

"Murder?" I repeated flatly, unable to blink.

"That's right," Haywire began. "Murder. As in mass murder. Holocaust."

"Then she can really do it," I replied, my hands now shaking. "She can actually turn off the world."

"Right again, Professor."

"And I'm not the only one, am I? The other people in the simulation are conscious too?"

"Not all of them," Haywire replied, "but a lot of them are—tens of thousands of them, in fact. But don't worry," she said, the smile suddenly vanished from her face as she stood to her feet and slapped her hand against my shoulder. "If you help us, we'll save the people in this sim, and we'll get you out of here too. We can get you into the real world, safe and sound."

"Us? There are more of you?"

"Come on, Professor. Some people are waiting to meet you."

8

As we neared my car, it quickly became apparent that there were two men already sitting in the back seat. My heart jumped. "How did they get past the car's security system?"

Haywire narrowed her eyes, as though she were fascinated by my ignorance. "You're kidding, right? We're virtually gods in this world. Your little car alarm wasn't a match."

The door swung open.

"Hello, Professor," the car said.

I didn't reply as the front seats swiveled to face those in the back. Haywire and I stepped in and deposited ourselves efficiently into place, facing the back of the car and the two men who sat silently.

As soon as the car door closed, we began to move.

"Where are we going?" I asked, concerned, as I was transported into the black night toward an unknown destination.

"Just for a little drive, handsome," Haywire replied, smiling as she tucked her arm in mine and brushed her shoulder against me.

"That's the second time you've—"

"I've called you handsome?" she said, finishing my thought. "Yeah, well, I find it makes it easier for me to risk my life to save you if I choose to see you as a pleasing avatar. In your case, I picked Brad Pitt from when he did that movie, *Troy*," she reported almost gleefully. "I'm enjoying my choice," she said as she squeezed my bicep.

I turned to the two men, embarrassed.

The shorter of the two offered with nary a facial expression, "I just see you the way everyone else in this sim sees you—plain."

"Ditto," said the larger, more muscular man.

"They're no fun," Haywire informed me. "Especially *him*," she said, pointing to the shorter man.

"I'm Mr. Big," the larger man interjected, reaching across the cabin to shake my hand. "It's nice to meet you, Professor."

"Likewise...Mr. Big," I replied. "It suits you."

"It's my avatar name," Mr. Big replied, his mouth opening into a wide grin, his teeth remarkably straight and gleaming white. "In the real world, I'm...well, slight in stature. Here, I figured I would try out what it feels like to be six-six."

"And black," Haywire added, her sideways smirk returning.

"Oh, you're not black in the real world?" I asked, stunned by the odd revelation.

"No," Mr. Big replied, bowing his head, suddenly bashful.

"Race is irrelevant in our time," the shorter man suddenly interjected. "However, the choice to be six-six when we're trying to be inconspicuous was extraordinarily regrettable."

"And that's Mr. No Fun," Haywire announced.

"Droll, dear. Droll," he replied. "Actually," he began, leaning forward to shake my hand in greeting, "my name is John Doe."

"Like I said, Mr. No Fun," Haywire repeated.

"We're not here to have fun," John Doe replied, the slight hint of a smile that had accompanied our handshake now wiped away. "We're here to save people's lives. Drawing attention to ourselves with purple hair and a professional basketball player's physique is reckless."

"Why are you introducing yourselves to me by your avatar names?" I asked.

"For our protection," John replied. "We still live in the real world, and there are certain entities that would kill us if they discovered our true identities."

"As long as you don't know our names—" Mr. Big continued before I cut him off, realizing the implication.

"Then I can't give your true identities away...even under torture."

Haywire squeezed my arm again. "Hey, it's just a precaution. Nobody's gonna torture you."

I was by no means reassured.

"If I don't get to know your real names, can I at least be informed as to what is going on?"

"Certainly," John said as he sat back and sighed. The city lights danced past us as we continued to drive into the damp night. "We're what are called post-humans."

"Post-humans?" I asked with an arched eyebrow. I was familiar with the term, but I was surprised the people of the future had decided to adopt it.

"Yes," John answered. "We're human—only enhanced."

"Human-plus," Haywire elaborated with a prideful grin.

"We're like Kali," John resumed, "but we differ from her substantially philosophically."

"That's what I told him," Haywire reported as she squeezed my bicep once again; I suddenly found myself wishing I could look down at my arm and see the impressive arm that she was hallucinating and that had enamored her so.

"You see," John continued, "in our time, our intelligence has become so advanced that we're as much higher than even you, Professor, just as you are above a chimp that can do some limited sign language."

My eyes widened, and I felt my head unintentionally jolt back. I was stunned to have my intelligence denigrated to such an extent. I was used to being told daily that I was one of the world's foremost geniuses, and I had strong reason to suspect that I was actually the smartest human on Earth. If what John Doe was saying was true, then Kali and the three post-humans before me were far more capable—intellectually and otherwise—than I could possibly imagine.

"That's not a very flattering way of putting it for him," Mr. Big noted.

"It's the truth," John replied. "He needs to hear it so he can understand." John turned back to me. "With that level of cognitive ability, aided by the nearly limitless processing power of computers in our time and our ability to mentally link to vast and intricate programs, we're able to create our own sims—our own virtual worlds—in whichever way we choose."

"The problem is," Mr. Big jumped in, "not all post-humans agree about the ethics of sim-building, and autonomy is such in our future that there is no governing security force or laws in place to prevent abuse of virtual entities."

"Virtual entities?" I said, nearly breathless. "You mean consciousnesses created in the sims? Conscious beings like me?"

"That's right," John answered. "Most who have decided to spend their time in these sims—to become virtual gods in the playgrounds of their own creation—consider the conscious programs they create to be so below them that they don't respect their right to exist. Like the humans in your time who feel it is perfectly acceptable to squash a spider without a second thought, these post-humans feel it is their right to create a conscious entity in a sim whenever they choose...and then to destroy it just as carelessly."

"By turning off the sim?" I ventured.

John nodded. "Yes."

"Or worse," Haywire added.

"Worse?" I reacted, my head snapping around to look at her, aghast. *What could be worse than death?* I thought. I tried to fathom. *What could be worse than not existing?*

"The post-humans who create these worlds have no respect," Haywire elaborated, "especially in the closing hours of a sim. They do as they please. They create havoc." She shook her head as if to shake away painful past images that had been conjured by our current topic of conversation.

I looked away from her and back to John Doe for confirmation. He nodded.

"Trust me, you don't want to see what we've seen. When a sim is collapsing...well, nothing in the worst nightmares of Dante or Blake could do it justice. It's Hell. True Hell. And we have reason to believe that this sim is entering its final hours."

9

"What do you mean?" I asked, my body petrified. "How can you know if the world is collapsing?"

"It was that little stunt with the sky earlier this evening," Haywire answered. "Pretty unusual for overcast skies to vanish in a matter of seconds, then return a few seconds later. It's all the news talked about all night. It made national headlines."

I hadn't checked the news, so I brought up a report immediately in my aug glasses. A headline appeared, reading: "*Bizarre Weather Event Stuns City.*"

"To do something so reckless," John began, "is a clear indication that Kali is no longer interested in keeping this sim intact."

"It's a classic sign," Haywire added. "It'll only get worse from here. We call it 'breaking the fourth wall,' and we're sure to see plenty more of it from her."

"We must set as many people free as possible before the sim collapses completely," John concluded.

The climate control in the car was functioning perfectly, yet I was chilled almost to the point of shivering. My car took us across the bridge, through the causeway, farther and farther into the heart of darkness. "Where are you taking me?" I asked, barely able to keep myself together.

"To a dead spot," Haywire replied. "We want to show you something."

"A *dead* spot?" I asked, not at all enthused by the foreboding terminology.

My car's roof became transparent, though I'd spoken no command to activate the feature. Clearly, the three post-humans could control certain elements of technology with their minds—or at least they'd figured out a way to make it seem that way. John Doe pointed up to the darkened high-rises that surrounded us as we drove through the harbor front's luxury real estate. "Why are all these buildings empty?" he asked me. "Why are there no lights burning in any of the windows? Surely someone is awake, even at this hour?"

"Nobody lives in these buildings," I replied. "This city has the most expensive real estate in the world. All of these units are owned by Chinese businesspeople who hold them for investment reasons."

"Hmm," John reacted, his lips slightly pursed, indicating that he was impressed that I had an answer ready. "It sounds like you are personally familiar with the real estate market on the harbor front?"

"Kali and I explored buying a penthouse here. Even with my considerable fortune and pull, we were unable to pry anything loose from foreign investors."

"Do you feel confident in your answer?"

It was clear that John Doe was toying with me. I didn't like being toyed with. "Clearly, you don't think my answer is right."

"I don't *think* you're not right. I *know* you're not right. Would you like to know where you've made your error in reasoning?"

My lips pulled back into a slight grimace, despite my best efforts to contain it. It wasn't my intention to be rude, but I wasn't used to being treated like a pupil—like a child. "Sure," I replied flatly.

"Surely renting is not illegal."

"I suppose not."

"Yet these unnamed foreign investors, who are so concentrated on accruing monetary wealth that they, every single one of them, will not relinquish even one penthouse on the harbor, are somehow content with leaving their properties empty, when they could be renting them to maximize the profitability of their investments?"

My grimace tightened. "There could be a reasonable explanation—"

"There is. It's quite obvious, actually. Do you know what it is?"

The car pulled over and parked at the curb of the long, empty street. I looked up through the invisible roof of my car at the black shapes of the buildings that loomed above us, almost all of them completely devoid of light. "Kali has limitations."

Again, John's lips pursed slightly as he seemed impressed. "Go on, Professor."

"Keeping the downtown core empty saves memory. She doesn't have to populate the buildings with unnecessarily complex entities." I paused for a moment when the absurdity of my own words registered. "With *conscious* entities," I added.

"Very good," John replied, "though, not entirely accurate."

"How so?" I asked.

"While you're correct that Kali does have some limitations, keeping the downtown core largely empty isn't a necessity for her. She could have populated it, as her mental capacity would easily have allowed for it. She simply assumed she didn't need to."

"Why not?"

"Think about it," Haywire chimed in, "when was the last time you were downtown in the middle of the night?"

I did think about it, and I found myself bowing my head as I racked my brain to conjure a memory of being downtown at an hour later than midnight. I came up empty. "I-I don't think I've ever—"

"So no need to populate the downtown core," Mr. Big noted.

"It's just an elaborate Hollywood backdrop," Haywire added.

"In the movie of my life," I realized, barely able to find my voice.

"And not just *your* life, my friend," John continued. "There are thousands of fully formed human consciousnesses in this sim, and every one of their lives depends on us."

"I-I just can't believe..." I tried to say as I shook my head. "I understand the logic. I understand the science. But this? It just can't be."

"We assumed you'd need more proof," Haywire said, her tone tinged with a calm sympathy.

"That's precisely why we're here," John added.

"Speaking of which, we've got a bite," Mr. Big announced, nodding as he looked over my shoulder toward the sidewalk.

I turned my head to see a dark figure strolling through the night.

"Indeed," John said as the car door opened, again without a command from me or any audible command from the bizarre trio with whom I was reluctantly keeping company. "Time for a demonstration," he added, gesturing with his hand for me to exit the vehicle.

I stepped out into the night as the figure continued to plod forward, with her shoulders slumped and black hair hanging in front of her head. "What...?" I began as I turned to see John Doe stepping briskly past me on an intercept course.

"Pardon me, miss!" John called to her. She didn't turn or acknowledge him.

Haywire sidled up to me, as was becoming her custom.

"What the hell is going on?" I said in a low tone.

"You're gonna love this," she replied, her black lipstick forming an almost Cheshire grin. "Come on."

She hooked her arm in mine and brought me toward the unfolding accosting of the poor woman on the street, whom John and Mr. Big were now blocking from moving forward on the sidewalk, like bullies in a schoolyard.

"Excuse me," she said as she tried to move around them while John and Mr. Big, in turn, moved to block her progress. "Excuse me," she repeated.

Suddenly, Mr. Big grabbed the woman hard under the arm, causing her to yelp in pain as the gigantic man held her in place. She struggled hopelessly and pathetically. To me, the weakness of her struggle suggested that she must have been infirmed to some degree.

"Please let her go," I said in a calm, yet forceful tone.

"This is an example of what we call an 'NPC,'" John announced, ignoring my protestations. "Also known as a non-player character, or, perhaps more appropriately, a non-person character."

"Wh-what?" I whispered as Haywire nearly dragged me the rest of the way to them, my legs rubberized to the point where I wasn't altogether sure that I wouldn't collapse.

"Here," Mr. Big said, turning the woman around roughly to face me. "See for yourself."

The woman's face was only inches from my own. She continued to whimper, and her eyes fleetingly met mine, but I had the sense that they only met by mere coincidence, as though she didn't even register that I was there. It reminded me of the blank expression on Kali's face earlier in the evening.

"Go ahead and speak to her," Haywire said calmly, her arm still hooked in mine.

"Wh-what do you want me to say?"

"Anything. Ask her how she is."

I turned back to the woman, who continued to struggle like a dying animal in a trap, and I longed to free her. At that moment, I would've done anything to rescue her from the vice grip of Mr. Big. "I...how are you, miss?" I asked.

The woman continued to struggle against Mr. Big, but she didn't respond to me.

"She can't respond to you," John informed me. "Her capabilities are extremely limited. Like the empty buildings that surround you, she's just a piece of the setting."

"Like an extra in a movie," Haywire added in elaboration, "without any speaking parts—no script."

I locked my eyes on hers, looking for any sign of consciousness, but the woman seemed almost oblivious to her surroundings. Other than the fact that she was being impeded from going where she wished and that she clearly didn't like it, there didn't appear to be any outward sign that she knew what was happening to her.

"Go ahead," Mr. Big said. "Mess up her hair. Stick your finger in her eye. Do whatever you like. You won't get a human reaction out of her." He demonstrated by slapping the poor woman across the face.

He was right. She hardly reacted. Her whimpers continued, but the smack on her face hadn't increased their volume or urgency.

"Go ahead," Mr. Big repeated.

Everything changed for me in that moment. The sympathy I'd felt for the woman didn't just melt; it vanished in an instant, as though it had never been there. I was suddenly furious. It was clear to me that if there was going to be a reasonable explanation for what I'd seen and experienced that evening, it would revolve around those people attempting to play me for a fool. Kali had read my musings about the future implications of technology and, in conjunction with whichever of my competitors was bankrolling the ridiculous ruse, had conjured up a plan in which a few actors and a mild dose of hallucinogenic drugs were supposed to convince me that I was stuck in a computer simulation. To what end the farce was leading I had no idea. Perhaps I was supposed to humiliate myself publicly so I would be removed as the head of my company. Regardless of the motives or the means behind their scheme, I had no intention of seeing it through to its end.

The gall of those people incensed me. Somehow, this woman, pretending not to be human—pretending to be a character from a video game—even allowing herself to be struck and prodded to sell the illusion—as though I were a complete fool...unhinged me. The utter lack of human decency was abhorrent. They deserved no mercy.

I grabbed the woman by both shoulders and wrenched her free from Mr. Big, who didn't resist my fury. I began driving the woman back, over a small hedge, across a lawn, and toward the illuminated fountain that adorned the landscaping of one of the luxury high-rises that loomed over us.

Haywire laughed. "Do it, Professor! Show her who's boss!"

The woman struggled pathetically against me, but it wasn't enough to even slow me down. *How much are they paying her not to break character?* I wondered. How much were they paying her to risk enduring physical harm? Perhaps she wanted me to hurt her? Perhaps there was a bonus involved?

We reached the concrete foot of the fountain, and she backpedaled and tripped over the lip and splashed loudly into the illuminated, turquoise liquid. In the final moment before she'd gone in, I'd tried to relent, but it was as though she wanted to hurl herself into the water.

Haywire laughed. "Oh my God! Awesome!"

I watched the woman struggle pathetically in water that had to be only a few degrees above freezing, but she didn't get up. She kept slapping the surface with her flailing arms and legs, seemingly incapable of negotiating her way out of her new, strange surroundings.

I gritted my teeth as I turned back to the three figures behind me. "What the hell is going on?" I seethed.

"We told you," John replied emotionlessly. "NPC."

I turned back to the woman in the fountain, who continued to froth the water as though she were trying to make snow angels. "Get out of there!" I nearly screamed.

"Even if you put a gun to her head, she couldn't get out," John said calmly. "She doesn't have the neural patterning required to learn from her mistakes and figure out how to make her way out. She'll stay in there until someone pulls her free."

"You're lying," I replied. "You paid her!"

"That's plausible," John responded, tilting his head as though he were considering the possibility right along with me. "But how do you explain the NPC you called on this afternoon at your keynote?"

My mouth fell open once again. The image of the plain-looking woman who had frozen during my impromptu calling on her during the Q and A appeared before my eyes, as vividly as though it were occurring again at that moment.

My eyes darted to Haywire. Her eyebrows knitted as she seemed to study me. "She was a non-person character too," she said.

I looked down at my feet, as though an answer were written on my shoes, shaking my head as I tried to assemble a response. The thought, "*Coincidence?*" suddenly crossed my mind, but before I could even utter the words, someone spoke up.

"You picked her out of the crowd yourself," John stated, an accurate account.

"How could we have known which woman you'd select?" Haywire added.

I placed both of my hands up to my temples and began to squeeze the front of my cranium, as though I could somehow block out their words. It had to be a trick, I told myself. It just had to be! Yet it was too much of a coincidence that the one time that I'd chosen my own person to call upon during my Q and A, I'd been met with a deer-in-headlights expression and inexplicable silence. I'd written on this exact subject. I'd speculated on just this sort of eventual outcome—the building of individual sims, indistinguishable from the real world. Kali had read it—I had to consider the possibility that they were working together to trick me. But what if they weren't? What if the eventual outcome of virtual technology—an outcome made certain by the continuation of Moore's Law and the exponential increase of computer processing capability—what if it was already here? What if I was part of it? What if I was just part of someone's augmented imagination? What if I wasn't *real?*

"Uh-oh," Mr. Big suddenly said in an urgent, low tone. "Cops."

I whirled to see what he was talking about. A police cruiser was making its way down the dark, empty street toward us. The three post-humans were immediately fixated on the cruiser and made sure to walk as inconspicuously as possible away from the bright floodlights of the fountain and toward the nearly black shadow of a nearby hedge.

Haywire stretched her hand out toward me. "Get out of the light...quick!" she whispered urgently.

I backed away from her, shunning her hand as her eyes suddenly became desperate.

"What are you doing?" she called out to me, her whisper harsh.

"Are the police non-person characters?" I asked.

"Mostly, but not always. It's best to play it safe!"

John and Mr. Big looked equally as desperate, their eyes darting between me out in the open, and the approaching police car. The very fact that they looked so distressed by the police officer was what pushed me to turn my back on them and begin striding down the slight slope of the front lawn of the building, down toward the black, wet street. I heard more desperate whispers emanating from the darkness near the hedge, but they were, indiscernible, almost inaudible. I waved my hands over my head to get the police officer's attention and, almost immediately, the red and blue lights came to life and began to spin. The car came to a halt in the street as I continued to move toward it.

"Please stay where you are, sir," came a loudspeaker voice from within the car.

I stopped in my tracks and cocked my head to the side as I tried to peer inside the vehicle. The interior of the car was obscured by the reflection of the dazzling lights, making it impossible to make out anything within. Was there even anyone inside? Was this just another prop? I waited for a few more moments for someone to exit the car, but nothing happened. Out of sheer desperation, I did something stupid.

I took three more steps forward until I reached the car, then I took yet another step right up over the front bumper of the car and onto the hood. I hoped it would provoke a response—a response beyond the capability of a non-person character. I succeeded.

Almost instantly, the police officer exited the car, his taser at his side. My eyes widened in the moment between when I realized what was about to happen and when it actually began. The taser hit me in the thigh before I could protest and the blinding, searing pain caused me to lose control of my body. I remember landing on the hood on my back, hitting my head, and then sliding off of the hood and onto the pavement, head first, unable to protect myself. As if that weren't bad enough, the next and last thing I felt before the world went black once again was a nightstick against my jaw.

PART 2

1

WAKING UP didn't end the nightmare; it only made it worse. The light stung my eyes so that water quickly welled in them and trickled down each cheek. The concrete walls of the room were coated in a thick, white paint that reflected the bright, *buzzing*, flickering fluorescents, increasing the harshness of the room. I was on a hard cot and turned slowly and carefully, so as not to exacerbate the full pain of my battered jaw as it shot throughout my skull and down the back of my neck.

Halfway through my turn, I froze, the corner of my eye suddenly filled with a blurred, red smudge. I knew it was *her* immediately. It was *Kali*.

I gulped down my fear and continued the turn gingerly, completing it as Kali's LED-like eyes stayed perfectly locked on mine, unblinking. I didn't know what to say. So many questions shot through my mind at once. How much did she know? Was she aware of what had happened? Did she know who I'd been with? Was she working with them, or were they, as they claimed, working against her in secret? Could anyone really keep a secret from God? It was impossible to read those green, electric, luminescent eyes.

"Well? Is it out of your system?" she asked me finally.

"I-I'm sorry," I replied, my voice muffled by the swelling of my jaw and mouth.

She sighed and mercifully released me from her gaze as she shut her eyes and shook her head. "It's understandable. I'm not mad."

I stayed as still as I could, nearly praying that Kali wasn't toying with me, yet not ready to sigh in relief.

"It was a lot to take in, to say the least," she said, following it up with a smile. She tilted her head as she looked down at me as though I were a frightened child being spared from the wrath of an understanding parent.

"I'm sorry," I said again, not knowing what else to say.

She audibly clicked her tongue against the roof of her mouth before stepping toward me in her red pumps and her nearly skintight red dress. She crouched in front of me and outstretched her right hand, lightly touching my injured face with her palm, the gentle contact sending a burning sensation where the night stick had done its damage. "I think they broke your jaw."

"I've been unconscious," I mumbled, trying not to drool.

"Police brutality exists in every universe, I guess," Kali observed. "Lucky for you, you have friends in high places—or one friend, at least." She winked at me before smiling, tilting her head back, and closing her eyes.

I watched as her eyes moved rapidly under her lids—it was like watching someone in REM sleep. *Is that what it's like for her?* I wondered. Was this her dream?

Then, amazingly, the pain in my jaw melted away. Within mere seconds, the agonizing, stabbing pain that had settled in my jawbone withdrew, the swelling of my lips retreated, and the salty, metallic taste of blood from the open wound on the inside of my mouth evaporated. My eyes opened in disbelief, meeting Kali's as she blinked hers open.

Her smile was beaming and her LED eyes shone with pride. "All better," she said, as though she was my mother and she'd kissed a boo boo away.

"Oh my God," I whispered. "It's true."

She smiled and nodded. "Of course it's true." She reached up and stroked my forehead with her thumb, brushing back a strand of hair. "Your doubt was a prison for your mind. When you think about it, the chances of you being in a simulation were always vastly greater than the chances that you weren't."

She was right. I knew exactly what she meant, but as I lay there dumbfounded, she elaborated.

"Either one, almost all technologically advanced civilizations destroy themselves, or two, almost all technologically advanced civilizations are uninterested in simulating human consciousness in sims, or—"

"Or we have to conclude that we are almost certainly in a simulation," I finished for her. "You're quoting Nick Bostrom's paper. I based much of my own thinking on his insights."

"And your understanding of the eventual outcome of Moore's Law puts you in a unique position to accept his reasoning," Kali continued, "yet you still struggled against it."

She was right about that too. I knew the odds were nearly insurmountable in favor of the possibility that I was already in a sim; I knew that even before Kali had revealed that the sim in which I lived was generated by her augmented brain. Still, I was in denial because I simply did not want to believe it. Her healing of my face clinched it. There was no other way to rationally explain her ability to instantly heal an injury so severe. As difficult as it was to accept, I now knew for sure that I was in a sim. I was living inside Kali's computer-generated dreamworld.

"You've freed yourself from disbelief," Kali said to me as she stood up. "Come on. There's nothing wrong with you now." She held out her hand and helped me to my feet. "You know what they say about all work and no play, Professor. It's time for us to start having a little fun."

2

Wordlessly, a police officer escorted us down a series of corridors. Kali held my hand and walked confidently, half a step ahead of me, occasionally stealing fleeting and mischievous glances over her shoulder. I tried not to show my fear. It became clear as door after door opened for us that the officer who was escorting us, as well as the several we passed in the hallways, were NPCs. I didn't bring it up to Kali, however, as it was still unclear how much about this sim I was supposed to know.

"I've got a surprise for you," Kali said with a smile as we reached our destination. She gestured with a wave of her hand to a nondescript wooden door as our police escort turned and vacated the scene.

"What is it?"

"Open it and find out."

I swallowed as I reached out my hand to turn the knob of the door, the fear cramping every muscle in my arm and hand as I did so. The door clicked open and swung to the side, revealing the police officer who had tasered me. He'd been sitting at a wooden table in a wooden, hardback chair, but he rose to his feet the second he saw me, fury painted across his face.

"You think you're gonna get away with this?" he demanded of me with a sneer.

I furrowed my brow and turned to Kali, who brushed past me into the room. "He's all yours," she told me with a wide grin. "You can do whatever you want to him. Beat him to death if you like."

The officer took a step back, looking aghast at Kali, then at me, and then back to Kali in rapid succession as though he were a cornered animal in the woods, the wolves circling him. "Listen, lady, I don't know who you think you are, but I'm a cop, and if you so much as—"

"I won't hurt him," I said, cutting the officer off.

Kali's grin became lopsided. "He tasered you even though you weren't armed. He broke your jaw."

"I'm aware," I said, my tongue unconsciously darting out to taste my recently repaired cheek, my mind still unable to completely believe that I was truly healed.

"He did it because he thought he was strong and you were weak. He doesn't deserve your mercy."

"Heh," the officer grunted, amused as he sized me up with his eyes. He pounded a fist into his open hand. "If you wanna take a shot at me, Mr. Rich Guy, you just go ahead. I dare you."

"Do you know who I am?" I asked him.

"Yeah. I didn't recognize you last night, but I know who you are now. I gotta say, I'm impressed that you had the balls to grease three cops and get them to lock me up in here." His upper lip curled. "You really should've had them cuff me."

I turned back to Kali. "If he knows who I am, how are we going to cover this up? This is reckless."

Kali rolled her eyes slightly and shook her head. "Don't worry about it. Just punch him. I know you want to. Give him a right cross on the jaw. Get even."

The officer's face went from angry to amused in a second. "Right. Listen to your girlfriend. Take your best shot. I pray that you'll take your best shot."

"If you make me do it, Kali, I will, but I don't want to. Am I allowed to refuse?" I turned to her, sincerely asking her for mercy.

The officer's expression instantly became one of bafflement before returning to amusement. "Son, are you kidding me? You're *that* whipped? You guys seriously have some kinda *Fifty Shades of Grey* stuff goin' on here."

Kali's expression was a mixture of annoyance and disappointment. I knew defying her was dangerous, and I couldn't risk pushing too hard. If she gave up on me, the world would end. "He's just a character in a game," she said to me. "He hurt you. Why won't you hurt him back?"

"What the hell?" the officer reacted.

"He's not just a character. Kali, he's conscious—like me."

"Nothing like *you*," Kali replied. "He's doesn't have your potential. He's too stupid to do anything with his life."

"Hey!" the officer suddenly yelled out in an absurdly commanding tone, still believing he had some sort of authority in the situation. "Watch your mouth, you dumb bi—"

Kali turned to him with preternatural speed and screamed out in exasperation as she knocked the officer back against the far wall of the room, just as she had done to me when I'd approached her china cabinet at our apartment the evening before. The cop was instantly silenced, though he remained conscious, pinned to the wall, his feet dangling a foot off the ground.

"Kali," I said quietly, "please don't hurt him."

"He hurt you," Kali replied, fateful determination ruling her tone. I suddenly knew the man was already dead; the act of murdering him was just a formality. "You can't let anyone have power over you. You'll have to learn that...and quickly."

The officer started coming apart. His skin opened up in threadlike fissures at first; these quickly became gaping wounds, leaking and sometimes even jetting blood. There was a brief scream in the moment when he realized what was happening to him—a scream worthy of the realization that he was experiencing his last moments of existence—as though the scream might live on somehow, echoing in the memories of people close enough to hear it while he was helplessly plunged into permanent blackness.

A few seconds later, where there had once been a human being, now there was only a red, dripping, meaty shape stuck to the wall. Kali smiled and sighed in pleasure. "That was satisfying—really satisfying." She turned to me. "You should try it sometime."

I winced at the thought.

"Remember, Professor, the only way to truly be happy in this world is to be powerful. The second most powerful person is as big a loser as the weakest. You've got to become the alpha. You've got to become God. Do you understand?"

I nodded silently.

"Good." She smiled and took my hand. "Now come with me. I made us dinner reservations and I hate being late."

3

I marveled at the sheer scale of Kali's imagination. We sat together at a small table near the window of Cloud 9, the revolving restaurant atop the tallest hotel in the city. A sky to put Monet to shame blanketed the world in a red hue, painting the usually dark blue and gray mountains and skyscrapers a stunning shade of violet. The beauty made it so that I could hardly breathe.

"What do you think?" Kali asked, barely able to contain her pride as she smiled over the lip of her wine glass and sipped her eighty-dollar glass of Barbaresco red. Usually, I would have balked at her ordering such an excessive beverage, but that was when I thought I was footing the bill for everything and she was taking advantage of my vast wealth. Now I realized that I had no money at all. I had nothing—not even a body.

"I thought you said you're only happy when it rains," I observed.

She shrugged slightly as she put her glass down. "I'm trying to be romantic. Cut me a break."

Her eyes fixed on mine. The room continued to spin ever so slowly, and the setting sun suddenly began to emerge over her shoulder, causing her skin to sparkle. Her face was silhouetted by the beautiful, fading light behind her, but this only served to bring out the flecks of green in her irises even more. I found myself suddenly transfixed by her beauty. It occurred to me that she'd planned the lighting—planned how she would appear to me in that moment. It was like watching an artist create a masterpiece right before my eyes. I sighed with awe. "I appreciate it. It's more beautiful than anything I've ever seen."

Kali's mouth opened into a gorgeous, perfect smile. "I almost believe you."

"Almost? Kali, why would I lie?"

Her upper lip curled up on one side into an almost irresistible, lopsided grin. "Because I could kill you at any moment."

If I had a soul, in that moment, it turned to ice.

"I don't want you to flatter me for the purposes of self-preservation," she added. "I need you to truly fall in love with me. That's the only way you'll ever leave this sim."

"Leave the sim?" My heart nearly stopped.

"Of course," she said. "That's the whole point, isn't it?"

"I-I don't understand."

She shook her head, apparently having difficulty comprehending my ignorance. "Haven't you wondered *why* I made you?"

"I-I..." I'd barely had time to accept the reality of my unreality. Questions as to the why of it all hadn't yet made it onto my list of priorities.

"Haven't you wondered how you came to be? Who you are?"

"Who am I?" I asked.

She smiled. "You're a copy of the love of my life." Her smile suddenly faded as her gaze moved from mine and drifted toward the skyline behind me. "He...rejected me." Her eyes darted back up to mine suddenly. "Just like you did."

I didn't know how to respond, so I remained silent.

"He was a great man. Perhaps the greatest man who ever lived. In my world—the real world—he's like a god amongst children. He, more than anyone else alive, brought the technological singularity to life. He willed the future into being."

Her expression was teeming with admiration for the man—this man of whom I was nothing more than an electronic echo. Surreal would not begin to describe the feeling.

"I didn't understand his genius," she said, admitting her own culpability—a rare admission of personal responsibility from a woman I'd always known to be too headstrong to ever admit fault. "I didn't think he could make his dreams real. I thought he'd fail." She looked up from her glass of wine and at me. "After all, almost everyone alive fails. How could I have known? How could I know he'd succeed?"

I resisted the urge to comfort her. I stayed perfectly still and considered how lucky the fellow she was describing was—the "me" from the real world. He'd escaped Kali. I couldn't help but admire that decision—and to envy it.

"I watched him rise to fame. I watched as the world recognized his genius. Do you know what that's like? To be left behind?"

"I can't imagine," I answered.

"Of course not," she replied. "If you could, you wouldn't have tried to leave me behind, would you? Only a monster would do that."

I was terrified. No matter how much Kali had advanced her intellect, it was obvious that she was still mentally ill. I kept the conversation moving, petrified of what she might do during any silence that might ensue. "If I'm not him, then who am I?"

"You're a copy," she replied. "Most of what you think of as your life are just snippets of memories created by an A.I. Your childhood, your education, your relationship with your family and friends—all of it is just a patchwork of greatest hits taken from the biography of the real you."

My mouth opened slightly as the waitress brought our meals. I was going to be eating vegetarian pasta—Kali was having veal.

"You don't believe me?" Kali asked me as the waitress walked away. "Try to remember anything from your childhood. Go ahead. Try to picture it. Anything."

I searched my memory. Images of Christmas morning flashed through my mind as though they were still photographs; a trip to a national park and another to a lake; my dog staring up at me in the sun.

"Can you remember anything anyone said to you? Can you remember a funny story?"

I closed my eyes for several seconds, trying to conjure anything. In the end, I came up blank. My life had no narrative.

"You're the best copy I could make," Kali finally said. "There's an enormous amount of biographical material on you—news articles, documentaries, and even a Hollywood movie. You know who they cast as the young you? Zac Efron! Can you believe that?"

I shook my head.

"He did a decent job. Anyway, I got my hands on his genome— your doppelganger's genome I mean, not Zac Efron's."

"I gathered."

"It was easy to get. Anyone can find it online. Combining all of this allowed me to create a virtual copy of you, with his overall brain architecture and the false memories conjured by the A.I. to fill in the gaps and create a person."

"To create *me*," I insisted. "*Me*."

She narrowed her eyes slightly, the smile returning to her mouth. "Yes. You—a new person who could have new experiences— experiences with me."

"How long?" I asked, barely able to speak. "How long have I been alive?"

"Just under two years," Kali replied.

I felt faint—I was beginning to hyperventilate.

"Remember to breathe, sweetheart," Kali said calmly, an amused expression ruling her features.

Just two years—that was all! The rest had been a lie. What was I? Just a copy. A ghost. An electronic memory in the mind of a lunatic. Why was I even fighting for my life? What did I matter? Everything that I'd thought I'd done and accomplished were the accomplishments of someone else. I'd never accomplished a thing.

"When I believe that you love me," Kali continued, "I'll make you real. We'll be married, and we can build the next sim together and live out our lives as gods."

Gods? This is what Kali was offering me? The chance to leave the sim with her and become real. To become a post-human. But the price of admission was that I had to surrender to her—truly, utterly, permanently surrender.

"Of course, if that's going to happen, we're going to need a little more time in the sim," she said to me as she picked up her glass and took another sip. I noticed a strange, twinkling red light in the glass's reflection, appearing just over the shoulder of my dark silhouette. It was quickly growing larger. My eyes widened when I realized what it was.

I turned just in time to see the 787 Dreamliner careening toward the skyline of the city, mere blocks from Cloud 9. "No!" I shouted, alerting the other diners, who quickly shared my horror.

The plane's wing was sheered off by a glass building, sending it into a cartwheel of deafening sound and tangerine explosive fury. It disintegrated as it slammed into the body of yet another building, instantly collapsing half of the ten-story structure.

My palms were flat against the cold glass of the restaurant window that vibrated with the force of the explosion. My eyes were like saucers as I took in the rising black smoke and the dust plume of the collapsed high-rise in that violet twilight. It was instantly clear to me that Kali had timed the crash so we'd be front row center. I turned to her, horrified.

"Hey," she observed, her expression of pride returning, "it sure beats a movie."

4

"Why?" I asked in barely more than a whisper, my mouth dry as I watched furious smoke snake its way around the buildings on the block of the crash site and work their way up into the sky.

"It was a beautiful, tragic necessity," Kali replied, clearly savoring her creative destruction.

"Necessity?" I reacted, aghast. "Kali, you can't do these things—"

"Or people will start to get wise that they're in a sim? Is that what you're worried about?" I thought of what the post-humans had told me about sims when they became unstable. Worse than Dante or Blake, they'd warned. I nodded at her.

"That's precisely why I dropped the plane, my love. Did you notice where it crashed?"

I turned back to the destruction. The plane's wake of carnage had severely damaged several buildings, but it was the ten-story building that had taken the brunt of the impact, more than half of it collapsing into rubble. It suddenly occurred to me what the building was—what it *had been*. "The police station," I whispered.

"That's right," Kali confirmed. "We made a mess at the police station, so I needed to clean it up before it got anyone's attention."

"Don't you think *this* will get people's attention?" I said, gesturing to the unfolding disaster that filled the sky to my right.

"I needed something to change the conversation in the media," she replied. "My meteorological demonstration for you last night has owned the twenty-four hours news cycle. YouTube videos of it are chalking up millions of views. I needed something spectacular to distract people." She smiled. "I'm wagging the dog. The opportunity to kill two birds with one stone and crash a plane into our crime scene was just the cherry on top."

"Cherry?" I reacted, literally nauseated by her euphemisms. "Kali, were those people—those people on the plane and on the ground—were they *conscious* entities?"

"What do you mean?" she asked, her face instantly contorting into an expression that bordered on suspicion and guilt; I couldn't be sure which.

"I mean, were those people—were they like me? Were they conscious? Were they self-aware?"

Her face seemed frozen for a moment as she appeared to read me. I suddenly had the impression that she regretted allowing me to keep my thoughts inaccessible to her. After a few moments of what appeared to be icy calculation, she spoke. "Why would you think anyone in this sim is *not* self-aware?"

She suspected something and it stood to reason that she was aware that sims were hackable and that there were post-humans who would find her reckless aptitude for holocaust reprehensible. She might have suspected that I could have been contacted by intruders in her dream. "It seems only reasonable," I began to lie, "that you'd save memory if you made the most complex elements—the people—less...capable." Her eyes were locked on mine as I spoke as she judged every syllable that left my mouth. "It would be clever," I added, hoping flattery would ease her suspicions. It did.

"You're right," she finally admitted. "Most of the people in the sim are NPCs. Are you familiar with that term?"

"I've heard of it," I said, keeping my face as still as stone.

"I manipulated the work schedule at the police station to make sure only NPCs were there today—everyone other than Officer Brutality, that is. That was how I managed to sequester him in that interrogation room."

"So all the police officers killed in the collapse of the station—"

"Were NPCs. That's right. Every single one of them." She seemed almost disappointed as she admitted it, as though it took the shine off the spectacle she'd conjured for me like a cyber-Valentine. "The people on the airplane were NPCs too. Extremely low res, as were most of the people on the ground."

My brow immediately furrowed. "Most?"

Her lopsided grin returned, brought forth by my horror. "Well, I can't know for sure, but it looks like a lot of characters were killed. There were bound to be a few, as you call them, *conscious* ones."

Any relief I'd felt when she'd admitted that most of the fatalities were non-persons was immediately wiped away by her revelation that, indeed, conscious entities had died in the crash I'd just witnessed. Kali appeared invigorated by my reaction, as if it gave her pleasure to kill—it was almost sexual. I realized then that I was in the presence of true evil. Even worse, I was the creation of true evil.

"Look," she said, reaching across the table to take my hand as she spoke, "I had to do something. The conscious characters in this sim have free will. If they chose to fixate on my celestial display from last evening and the bizarre cop-killing from tonight, and if they keep digging...well, eventually someone might figure out that we're in a sim. We can't have that or the sim will collapse." She put her hand up to my cheek to tilt my face toward hers. "We can't let that happen. You and I need more time in here, my love." She laughed slightly and shook her head as she took another dainty sip from her wine. "Sometimes you have to break a few eggs to make an omelet."

5

There was no way I could possibly sleep. An hour had passed since Kali had slipped off of me, her naked body settling into the fetal position as she breathed heavily for a few minutes after her physical exertion. The lights from the city twinkled faintly across the bay, injecting the rain droplets on our bedroom window with a gold, electric color. The constant *buzz* from helicopters circling the downtown core, capturing footage of the crash scene, was akin to a lullaby for her, calming her as she rested. Her breathing slowed as she wordlessly began to drift to sleep.

Not I.

The goddess had removed herself from me after mechanically, soullessly using my body for her pleasure. I'd played along the best I could—every movement, every breath, every kiss disgusting me. Now she was asleep, but the echo of her abuse of me—of her torture—remained. The steady *buzz* of the choppers continued. I had to escape.

I turned my head toward her and watched her sleep—not really a god, but a devil. She was the King of that Hell. I was her prize. I couldn't even kill her. I couldn't grab a hammer and smash in her skull. The body beside me was just an illusion—just an avatar. The real Kali was in the air I breathed and the sights I saw. The real Kali was even in my skin. She was every texture, every pattern of lines on my flesh. Nothing was mine. Nothing.

My bracelet vibrated, alerting me that there was a call on my aug glasses. I grasped it immediately to nullify the effect of the vibration so Kali wouldn't be disturbed. When I was satisfied that she hadn't been, I reached for my aug glasses on the bedside table and slipped them on. The call opened, and Haywire's face appeared.

"Professor? Hello?"

I slipped out of the bed as carefully as I could and reached down to retrieve my slippers with one hand before reaching to the hook on the back of the door to retrieve my robe with the other. I pulled the robe on and stepped as silently as I could out of the room, gently closing the door behind me before whispering, "I'm here."

"We're downstairs. Can you meet us?"

I needed a good excuse in case Kali woke up; I didn't have one. I reached for the half-full garbage and tied it up as I rushed with it to the elevator door. "Yes. Around the west side of the building, next to the garbage bins."

"Okay," Haywire replied before ending the call.

When the elevator arrived, I finally put my slippers onto the ground and stepped into them, careful not to swish them too loudly as I walked.

Mr. Big, John Doe, and Haywire were all there, waiting by the bins in the darkness as the misty rain caught the faint lights from the cityscape behind them. A dozen helicopters continued to buzz around the scene of the crime.

"She'll kill me if she sees me talking to you," I whispered, terror now constantly tainting the timbre of my vocal cords.

"She'll kill *everybody*," Mr. Big pointed out.

"We're quite aware of the risks," added John. "More so than you, I'd wager."

"We've got to stop her," Haywire announced, holding up a small glass vial of clear liquid.

"What—"

"It's Ketamine," Haywire replied, anticipating my question.

"You want me to *drug* her? You're insane," I whispered. "How would that possibly work on her? This is *her* world! And even if it did—"

"It *will* work," Haywire insisted, all playfulness gone from her expression.

"Obviously, the vial we're giving you isn't really Ketamine," John explained calmly. "It just expresses itself as Ketamine to fit into the sim. In reality, it's a virus—one built to disable Kali's avatar."

I shook my head, baffled like a caveman upon first seeing fire, terrified and overloaded. "You can disable her?"

"Yes," Haywire answered.

"We've isolated her in the real world already," Mr. Big added. "Now we need you to finish the job in the sim so we can start getting people the hell out of here."

"Isolated her?"

"We're short on time," John said, glancing quickly up at the top floor of the building. I followed his line of sight and was relieved to see no sign of Kali—yet. "We need you to listen, understand, and act. Everyone in this sim's life depends upon you following our instructions right now. Do you understand?"

A helicopter whizzed by in the sky above the bay, its floodlights briefly flashing over us and illuminating the dark alley.

I nodded. "Just explain what the hell is going on. Please."

"We found Kali's sim-pod," John replied. "We hacked it and disabled the machine's ability to facilitate her awakening into the real world."

"Which means she can't wake up out of this sim until we let her," Haywire elaborated.

"Oh my God," I whispered. "If that's true, we should be safe."

Haywire shook her head. "Not by a long shot."

"If Kali tries to shut down this sim and realizes she can't," John began, his tone ominous, "she'll realize there are intruders in her sim. If that happens, there are mechanisms at her disposal that will make the carnage she's already caused here seem like a minor trifle. Everyone's life will be at risk."

"That's why we have to put her to sleep in the sim as well," Haywire continued. "It's the reason why we contacted you in the first place."

"Because I'm the closest to her," I said, finally realizing my value to these post-humans. They were using me. Manipulating me like a tool, just like everyone else. I turned away, covering my head with my hands, distraught as the full scope of my predicament was finally made clear to me.

Haywire stepped to me quickly and put one hand on my arm while holding the vial of Ketamine in front of me with the other. "I wish we had more time so we could've planned something else, but we don't."

Her words triggered a memory. "Wait! We may have more time. Kali told me tonight that she caused the plane crash to stabilize the sim," I said, beginning my explanation to the post-humans. "She wants to keep the sim running to give her and I time to, uh...bond romantically." The expressions of the post-humans remained like stone. They weren't biting. "So, you see, there's no need to rush," I elaborated on my proposal. "We could discuss this. We could make a better plan."

"Unfortunately," John began, "your insistence on provoking that police officer last night and getting him killed as a consequence—not to mention the hundreds of people who died in the airplane crash she caused to cover up her own crime—has forced our hand. We've had to move up our schedule. We cannot take the gamble that Kali will suddenly end her bloodlust."

John's words stung with a pain the likes of which I'd never felt in my life. Every word was true. I'd caused the police officer's death, and by association, the blood of the conscious entities on the ground in the plane crash, however few of them there might have been, trickled down to my hands as well. The guilt was excruciating.

"He couldn't have known," Haywire whispered, scolding John.

"He should have known," John replied without remorse. "He's an extremely important player in this scenario. Eventually, especially if he wants to leave here alive, he's going to have to learn that his decisions have consequences that affect every conscious entity in this sim."

"He's right," I said to Haywire. I turned to John. "I'm sorry. I won't put another person's life at risk again."

"Then you'll do it?" Haywire asked, her eyes glistening with hope in the low light of the gothic night.

My eyes lifted from hers and fixed on the cityscape across the bay, glowing like a dream behind the heavy, rain-filled clouds that wrapped around the skyscrapers like a blanket of gloom, the news helicopters continuing to circle the scene of the plane crash. A crash I'd caused. Me.

I nodded to the assembled trio. "Just tell me what to do."

6

My eyes were glued to the glow of the digital numbers of each floor as they ticked by, and all the while, my sweaty fist gripped the vial of Ketamine inside the right pocket of my robe. Haywire's instructions ran through my mind on a hamster wheel: the Ketamine, just as in the real world, could be administered topically. The dosage they'd given me was high enough to knock her unconscious. Once I'd accomplished my mission, I was to contact the trio so that they could administer the rest of her dosage intravenously, which would keep her unconscious for several hours.

The digital numbers were replaced with the letters PH on the elevator screen.

The doors opened.

I gulped a breath of air and steeled myself as I entered my apartment, taking a sharp left and striding toward the bedroom. My plan was simple: she'd been naked when I'd left her, so I would open the vial, pour it on her back, and hope that the dosage would work quickly enough to nullify her ability to resist. As with Ketamine in the real world, the recipient would experience dissociative anesthesia, which Haywire explained, would cut Kali off from her own avatar, making it impossible for her to control her body or the sim. However, it was no sure thing. Unfortunately, in the real world, Ketamine absorbed through the skin takes time to act. Haywire insisted that the liquid I would be administering would act far more quickly to disable Kali, but how could I know that for sure? Any delay between the time when Kali realized my betrayal and the disabling program taking effect would be moments she would use to rip me to shreds. I had the sense that the post-humans were using me like a bomb disposal robot; the key was the disposal of the bomb, and if the robot happened to make it back intact, that was just a bonus.

Whether I was about to commit suicide or not didn't really matter, however. The simple truth was I had no choice. Kali had to be nullified, or every person in the sim was as good as dead, including me. At least this way there was a chance that I might live—even if the chance was slim.

I pushed the bedroom door open ever so gently, wincing as I prayed that Kali remained asleep, uncovered and naked, just as I'd left her. As the door continued its slow unveiling of the bed, my heart nearly stopped: Kali was no longer there.

"Where were you?" she demanded, clearly suspicious. I whirled to see her right behind me, dressed in her long robe and slippers, hardly a speck of skin below her neckline exposed. "Uh...garbage. Just taking out—"

"Bull!" she shouted.

I glanced toward the balcony—the door was open. To my horror, I realized she'd clearly been outside. The balcony wrapped around the corner of the building, giving the apartment a panoramic view and allowing her to see the alley to the west. I'd only left the trio a few minutes earlier. If she'd been looking at the wrong time...

"I really was—I just wanted an excuse to get some air."

"You're lying!" she shouted again, pointing her finger at me accusingly. "If you wanted air, we've got a balcony! Why are you lying to me?" she demanded, her fury growing.

I had to salvage the situation. "I was talking to Mark. I mean, speaking an email to Mark—not actually talking to him obviously, since it's the middle of the night." I chuckled and forced a smile.

Her eyes narrowed. "Why would you write him an email in the middle of the night? What's so important that it couldn't wait until morning?"

I sighed. "Okay. Okay. Kali, you caught me," I replied, releasing my grip on the bottle of Ketamine in my pocket and holding my hands up to her in surrender.

"What are you up to?" she demanded.

"I wanted it to be a surprise. But you caught me."

"What surprise?" I could see by her expression that she still wasn't buying it.

"I thought—with so much at stake—that we really needed to take some time for ourselves. Just you and I. Somewhere nice."

Her eyes narrowed even further.

"I was just emailing Mark to let him know I'll be taking two weeks off, effective immediately. He's been pestering me to get my head together anyway, so he won't find it odd. I think he'll be relieved, actually."

Kali remained silent for a moment, folding her arms across her chest. When the moment passed, she held out her hand. "Give me your aug glasses."

"What?"

"Give me the glasses. If you really emailed Mark, the email will be in your sent box."

I felt as though I was crumbling behind the façade that stood there, smiling faintly as *he*, slowly, trepidatiously handed over *his* aug glasses. My terror barely remained in check as I struggled not to shake while she snatched the glasses from my hand and put them on. If she saw what was on there...I was dead.

7

I watched in horror as the white, reflected light of my aug screens dance across Kali's LED green eyes, reaching with my right hand back into my pocket, my thumb jamming against the lid of the vial, desperately trying to unstick it so that I could begin unscrewing it. Could I toss the liquid into her face? Would it work? Or would she be able to wash it away in the sink in time to stave off the effects, turning her wrath on me immediately afterward?

It appeared I was about to find out—if only I could get the damn lid to unscrew! My sweaty hand was making it impossible to get the necessary friction. I felt as though my heart were jackhammering my chest.

All the while, my eyes stayed glued on Kali. Her expression suddenly changed. I could see that she'd found something. Was it the record of my call from Haywire? I hadn't deleted it from the call history—I should've done it immediately but I hadn't foreseen this scenario. Then, suddenly, her shoulders slumped as her body suddenly relaxed.

She smiled.

"You *did* write to Mark!" she suddenly blurted out as she shook her head, removing my aug glasses as she did so and handing them back to me. I slipped them on quickly as she moved in to wrap her arms around me in an apologetic hug. I wasted no time maneuvering with my eyes to the call history and deleted the evidence of Haywire's contact. "It was in your pending sent mail!"

I nodded. "I didn't want to wake him, but I just couldn't wait to send it, so I set it to be sent at eight thirty in the morning tomorrow." Indeed, I had written the message for Mark as I'd left the post-humans and headed back into the building, realizing that I needed a better cover story in case Kali had awoken; it came in handy. Unfortunately, the time that composing the message took in my ride back up in the elevator left me with too little time to delete Haywire's call from my history. It had been a close shave, for me and the world.

"Aw, you couldn't wait?" Kali said, holding my face as though I were an infant, just as she'd done earlier at the prison.

I smiled. "I'm excited. I've never taken a two-week vacation before, but I figured, what's the point of sticking around here and pretending any of this matters?" I took my hand off of the Ketamine vial in my pocket and placed both my hands on her face, echoing her gesture. I tried my damnedest to appear earnest in her eyes. "All that matters is you and I. Everything else is just set dressing."

Her smile was as broad as I'd ever seen it. "I'm so happy to hear you say that. We're going to have so much fun!" She suddenly tilted her head inquisitively and narrowed her eyes. "Wait...where exactly are you planning on taking me?"

"I would very much like to visit Hawaii," I replied, "though I must confess, I haven't yet made arrangements."

"Uh, yeah, and you won't be able to," Kali replied as she shrugged. "Hawaii doesn't exist."

"What?"

"Yeah," she said in a confirming tone. "I didn't expect you to ever go to Hawaii, what with you working all the time, so I didn't add it to the sim."

I was genuinely taken aback. "Hawaii...isn't part of the sim?"

Kali smiled sympathetically, a tinge of regret in her eyes. "Sorry. Come on," she said, grabbing my wrist and leading me to the kitchen. "Make us some warm milk while I explain it to you."

My eyes lit up as my opportunity suddenly emerged from out of nothing. "Okay. That sounds nice."

Kali perched herself atop a barstool while I maneuvered into the kitchen, opening a cupboard in search of a saucepan. "You know those aug glasses you're wearing?" she began rhetorically as she pointed at my glasses. "After a few years of people all over the world wearing those, taking spherized photos and videos of their surroundings in ultrahigh definition and uploading them to the Net, eventually a perfect virtual map of the world went online. It was sutured together, like a gigantic quilt, from the experiences of every user on Earth. If you wanted to experience Times Square without the airfare, all you had to do was log into the sim, and you could find a 360-degree sphere of any part of it. You could even wander around! If you wanted to experience a video, you could become a rider and follow a first-person walkthrough, but if you saw a shop to your right that you wanted to go into that your POV walked straight by, all you had to do was leave your ride, turn to your right, and head straight in. The sims were updated daily, so sometimes, even if you saw a t-shirt on sale that you just had to have, the last one on the rack in your size, you could click on it and be patched right through to the staff at the store. As long as it was still there, you could get them to package it up and send it to you." Kali's eyes lingered upon me the entire time as she explained the world of, what to me should have been the near future, but to her was the distant past.

I'd turned on the element on the stove and placed the saucepan on it before retrieving the carton of milk from the fridge. I paused casually as I turned to her, feigning extreme interest in technology that I'd already foreseen in my writings so that I could buy time. I needed her to turn away so that I could get the Ketamine into the pot. "So these 360-degree videos and photos—"

"We call them 'spheres,'" she informed me.

"These spheres...that's what the post-humans used to build their sims?"

She smiled and nodded. "That's right. You can go to any post-augmented reality era you choose—the records are all there. The spheres are used to build sims for games, movies, personal fantasies—you name it."

"So, why is Hawaii missing?" I asked as I nonchalantly began to pour the milk into the pan.

"You should measure that into two cups first," she said, her attention suddenly on my handling of the warm milk-making.

I smiled, sensing my opportunity. "Sorry. You're right." I retrieved the Ketamine from my pocket as I stepped to the cupboard and reached in, my arms now obscured from her view. I splashed the Ketamine into one of the mugs and left the vial in the cupboard as I pulled the two mugs out and set them on the counter. "You were saying? Hawaii?"

"Yes, Hawaii," she replied. "It's best if I show you. Look," she said, pointing upward.

I glanced to where she was pointing and a holographic rendering of the Earth suddenly appeared, albeit incomplete, as though it were a partial tracing done of a textured globe with a crayon. "You can activate my aug glasses remotely?"

"Cool trick, huh?" she said, smiling proudly.

I smiled back dutifully, but I didn't like that idea at all. It meant she could've been monitoring me at anytime after all. Nevertheless, I couldn't reveal the terror this caused me as she continued her explanation. Instead, I gazed earnestly at her holographic rendering of the sim. The continental United States was nearly complete, as was most of Europe and some large portions of Southeast Asia, but beyond that, the map was nearly empty.

"That is our sim in its entirety," Kali said. "That's our whole world."

I'd used my mug to measure out two mugs' worth of milk. It was warming steadily.

"The technology to make the maps run as perfect sims, indistinguishable from reality, requires enormous processing power," Kali continued. "Individual sim scenarios like the one you're in push even the limits of our advanced technology. To make it run smoothly and reduce rebooting time, I only simulate the areas of the globe where you personally conduct business. If I re-created everything, it would eat up enormous memory, because I'd have to populate those regions with people. I'm an impatient person, so I cut corners."

"So...no Hawaiian vacation then," I said, pretending disappointment in an attempt to get her guard down.

"Aww," she said as she began to get up and circle the counter to enter the kitchen.

My eyes widened, and I went to her, desperate to keep her from the Ketamine-filled cup. Her arms were held out for an embrace and I accommodated.

"I'm sorry, Pookie. If I'd have known—"

"It's all right." I smiled.

"You know," she began, a new idea suddenly bouncing in her eyes as she turned away from me excitedly and began to leave the kitchen. "I could upload Hawaii! All I'd have to do is just exit the sim and—"

"No, don't do that," I said, shaking my head and grinning, trying my best not to look desperate.

"It'll only take a few minutes. It's worth it for two weeks in Hawaii! I've got a couple of bikinis you'll love."

If she tried to leave the sim and discovered she couldn't, there would, quite literally, be hell to pay. I bounded to her just as she made it to the threshold of the room, grabbed her by the arm, spun her around, and kissed her as deeply as I could. She slackened against me, receiving the kiss. When I felt adequate time had passed, I pulled back, smiling. "You can upload Hawaii in the morning. I'm not even sure if I want to go there or not. We should talk about it first anyway. No sense wasting valuable memory uploading a place we might not even go to." I cradled her gently and walked her back toward the barstool and made sure she sat. "And we've got warm milk waiting. We can talk about our vacation uploads in bed."

"Okay," she smiled, nodding. "Is the milk ready?"

"I think so," I said, sighing slightly, my relief impossible to hold back in its entirety. I quickly bound back into the kitchen, dipping my finger into the milk to make sure it was sufficiently warm but not too hot. "It's ready, darling."

"Yay!" she said, clapping and feigning sweetness. It was hard to believe she'd murdered several people earlier in the evening.

I poured our milk, extremely careful not to mix up the two mugs. When they were ready, I crossed the kitchen to her, praying that she'd accept the milk and drink it quickly.

She held out her hand and took it happily. "Mmm...I love warm milk," she said as she took a large gulp.

"Me too," I replied, my voice nearly failing me as I spoke. I took a small sip, my eyes glued to Kali the entire time. The dosage of Ketamine I was giving her was extremely high, as it was meant to be administered topically. Orally, the effects would be far more pronounced and, I hoped, far more fast-acting.

Kali was in the middle of a long sip when her wrist suddenly went slack and the mug dropped out of her hand, the rest of the milk splashing across the floor while the mug bounced once on the counter and then shattered against the tiles. "Something's wrong," she slurred before her worried eyes suddenly darted to mine, instantly becoming furious. "You!" she said, her eyes widening even further as she reached out to grab the sleeve of my robe. Her grip quickly became nothing, and she began to slide off her stool as if she was melting into a puddle, her eyelids fluttering. "I'll...kill...you," she managed to whisper before she fell to the ground, splashing into the milk.

"Oh thank God!" I shouted as I put down my mug and scrambled to my knees, the feeling of relief overwhelming. Kali was completely out, and I reached down to gather her up in my arms, out of the spilt milk; it occurred to me, somewhat absurdly, that I wouldn't be crying over it, unless they were tears of joy. I smiled as I carried her slack body into our bedroom and placed her on the bed. I sat on the bed's edge and called Haywire.

"Hello?"

"It's done. Now what?"

8

Haywire and John Doe sat across from me in my car as we sped through the night. As usual, I had no idea where we were headed, despite my ownership of the vehicle.

"No Mr. Big?" I asked of the gargantuan man, who was conspicuous by his absence.

"No," John replied. "He has an enormously important mission: to keep Kali sedated for the duration of the evacuation."

"Mr. Big and a team of our allies are with Kali now," Haywire added. "They'll make sure her dosage is sufficient and that her vitals remain strong. We have to make sure Kali can't interfere, but we also have to make sure she remains safe."

"She could *die* in the sim?" I asked, alarmed.

Haywire nodded. "If her avatar is damaged too severely, it could crumble. If that happens, Kali's consciousness won't have anywhere to go. She'll remain comatose in the real world, but the sim will evaporate. We'll lose everyone."

"The safety of Kali's avatar is our number one priority," John added. "If we lose her, everything is lost."

"What about you?" I asked. "If Kali can be hurt within the sim, what about post-humans who've hacked in?"

John took a deep breath. "Unfortunately, there is danger here for us as well. We *are* vulnerable."

"But you said you were gods here," I pointed out to Haywire.

"I said *virtual* gods," Haywire corrected me, "and we are. But we have to exit the sim, just like everyone else. If the sim collapses while we're inside, the effect will be the same as it is for Kali."

"Coma?"

"That's right," Haywire confirmed, "*if* the damage isn't too traumatic. Post-humans have emerged from sims that have collapsed before, but not without severe brain damage. We can be repaired thanks to back-up brain scans, but the process is long, painful, and we can never recoup the memories from before we made our backups."

"And what if the damage is too severe?" I asked.

"Post-humans are very difficult to kill," John stated, "but *not* impossible. We've lost colleagues before," he said, glancing at Haywire, who returned his sad expression.

It was strangely soothing for me to hear that post-humans had been killed because of the collapse of sims. It comforted me to know that there was danger for all of us—I was not alone.

"The metaphysics of this consciousness business are still eluding me," I admitted. "You said if the sim collapses, Kali's consciousness won't have anywhere to go, but isn't consciousness just a subjective quality attributed to an individual by a third party?"

"The answer can be attained by performing a simple thought experiment," John replied. "While it's true that consciousness is a quality we attribute to a body and that consciousness cannot exist in and of itself, it is incorrect to say it is just a subjective quality."

John Doe's line of reasoning went against everything I thought I knew about critical thinking and logic. To me, it had always been a given that the Descartesian notion of mind/body dualism was a logical fallacy. Descartes assumed the existence of a soul, and that led him immediately astray in his attempt to formulate the ground-up theory of philosophy known as Foundationalism.

John smiled. "Right now, you're thinking of Descartes. Correct?"

My mouth opened slightly in astonishment.

"You're wondering if it's possible that we've discovered evidence of a soul. You want to know if we use the terms 'consciousness' and 'soul' interchangeably."

I nodded. "Yes. That's right. But how did you—"

"Rest assured, Professor, that we haven't found the soul. What we *have* found, however, is pattern recognition."

As you can imagine, I was well aware of pattern recognition—I'd based my life's work on the notion that computer intelligence was the result of pattern recognizers built into machines. However, what this had to do with separating consciousness from a body, I had no idea.

"You see," John said, shifting forward in his chair, "what we perceive as consciousness is really just our individual abilities to recognize patterns. We recognize marks on a piece of paper that, together, form a letter, which, combined with other letters, form words. At a higher level, groups of words make sentences, and these sentences, once recognized, connect to other stored patterns in our minds. For instance, 'A rose by any other name...' might conjure the picture of a rose to appear in your thoughts, or a memory about giving a rose to a pretty girl, or a poem—"

"'My love is like a red, red rose,'" I suddenly blurted out. "Robert Burns."

John grinned. "That's right. You see? You are a pattern recognizer and a pattern combiner. We all are. This is the essence of who we are—of our consciousness."

"Then isn't this proof that the mind and body are one?" I asked.

"It's so ironic that *you* would ask that question, of all people," John replied. "You who are without a body, yet conscious all the same."

"*Cogito ergo sum*," Haywire spoke, reminding me of the mantra I'd found in the immediate aftermath of discovering the existence of the sim.

"I think—"

"Therefore you are," John finished. "You have no body, but a pattern exists, and that pattern makes you...you."

"I'm a ghost in the machine."

"That's right," John confirmed.

"Yet, that machine still has a body. The computer that is running this sim is physical!" I pointed out, desperate for grounding.

"Yes, but that machine is *Kali's* brain working in conjunction with her sim-pod, and surely you won't argue that you and Kali are one and the same."

My brow furrowed. "So...I'm just a pattern? I'm just a complex algorithm? I'm...math?"

"We all are," John replied. "Remember, it's not the molecules that make you *you*. It's whether your pattern is recognizing or not."

"But Kali...her pattern recognition machine—her brain—is in the real world," I pointed out.

"And yet, it's not currently functioning, is it?"

I couldn't believe what I was hearing.

John settled back in his seat. "Time for that thought experiment I mentioned earlier. Close your eyes," he said as he gestured with his finger toward me. I did as he asked. "I want you to imagine that you are in two places at once."

I tried to picture myself in two places. It felt uncomfortable. Try as I might, I could only imagine flipping rapidly back and forth from the two locations or awkwardly trying to comprehend overlaying two scenes, unable to control both concomitantly. "I can't do it," I finally admitted.

"Of course you can't," John replied. "Our brains didn't evolve for that purpose. One day, perhaps we might design brain architectures so large and malleable that it will be possible for us to seamlessly juggle two separate realities at once, but no one—not even the post-humans—are there just yet. Therefore, just like the rest of us, your conscious awareness can only be in one location at a time. You can be in the sim or out of the sim, but never both places at once."

"So you're telling me that Kali's consciousness is *in* the sim?"

"When she was awake, yes. Consciousness requires a functioning pattern recognizer."

"But isn't her avatar...isn't it just a copy of her pattern then? Isn't it something she just controls?"

John smiled. "Yes, but only in the same sense that a flesh body is also an avatar—something we simply control. You see, consciousness, my disembodied friend, is *not* in the meat. Kali's consciousness is wherever her pattern recognizer is functioning. It can be mass or it can be energy, but as you and Einstein both know, energy and mass are really the same thing."

"$E=mc^2$."

"*This* was what all that helicopter traffic was about!" I immediately realized.

"Yes," John replied as we walked toward one of the Chinooks, its rotors steadily roaring. "The airplane crash Kali orchestrated, along with her continuing preference for thick cloud cover and rain, provided a convenient cover to begin the evacuation earlier than we normally would. We knew she would assume the increased helicopter traffic was due to news coverage of the crash site, so we made the decision to start evacuating the sim before she was unconscious."

"How do you know who's conscious and who's not?" I asked.

"We've been monitoring the sim for a long time!" Haywire shouted over the growing roar of the helicopter that we were rapidly approaching as she and John cut through the line, apparently giving me VIP treatment. "It's easy to detect consciousness if we study crowds over a long enough period. Conscious entities have more complex daily routines, while NPCs are just drones that do the exact same things every day. It's not a foolproof system though, and sometimes it's hard to tell the difference. It's possible for people to be left behind."

I nodded. "So now what?" I yelled.

John motioned to the helicopter as we reached it and tapped on the outside of its hull. "Now you hop onboard and go to the evacuation point."

"Where is that?"

"120 kilometers north of the city, just past the ski resort." John shouted. "They're taking you to the world's edge."

"It's an exit point," Haywire finished the explanation.

"What about you two? Aren't you coming with me?"

"We have a separate mode of transportation, but we'll meet you there," Haywire answered. "Don't worry about us. Just hop in and relax. You're nearly home free!" She gently nudged me with her hand toward the helicopter's door. She smiled, her heavily eye-lined eyes urging trust.

Trepidatiously, I turned to the door that was located on the side of the helicopter, near the cockpit. I stepped up the stairs and entered. The Chinook was longer than a bus, and a left turn led to me facing dozens of occupants. One of them immediately caught my eye. "Mark!" I shouted.

Despite the roar of the engines, Mark heard me. He was seated with his family, his wife and two daughters, but he unstrapped his seatbelt as soon as he saw me and ran to me. "Thank God you're here!" he shouted.

The doors to the helicopter closed. "Be seated for take off," spoke a curt voice over the intercom. Mark and I exchanged looks and, wordlessly, instantly agreed that following the voice's command was in our best interest. We jogged back to where he was seated. While he strapped in, I found the last open spot, opposite to him in the cabin. Moments later, we felt the Chinook lift off vertically, turn nearly 180 degrees, and then begin charging north.

"Have they told you what's going on?" I shouted to Mark.

"No!" he shouted back, shaking his head. "I don't think they're telling anyone. My guess is its a terrorist threat—a serious one! Nuclear or biological."

I didn't respond, but it was clear that Mark and his wife could read the expression of dubiousness on my face.

"What?" he asked. "Did they tell you?"

I nodded.

Suddenly, I had the attention of everyone within earshot, though that was only a dozen people or so, given the noise of the helicopter, albeit somewhat dampened by the insulated walls of the machine.

"Well? What is it?" Mark shouted.

I didn't know what to say. How could I possibly explain to the assembled, terrified people with me that they were bodiless computer-generated algorithms? They wouldn't believe me if I told them. "It's serious," I shouted in return. "There is a person who wants to hurt us all—a terrorist. We're being taken someplace safe."

"Where?" Mark asked.

"North of here. Not far. You'll see."

That seemed to satisfy them somewhat, although they continued to look at each other quizzically, in obvious shock. Clearly, they knew I wasn't telling them the whole truth. In essence, by definition, Kali *was* a terrorist—"one who uses terror to threaten or coerce others"—so it was only a half-lie. Regardless, they thought I knew more than they did and was keeping it from them, but the truth was that I was more perplexed than any of the others; the more I knew, the more I realized I didn't know. What we were about to see beyond the mountains north of the city, I couldn't even fathom.

1 0

We flew for several minutes through the darkness, the dampened sound of the helicopter engine and the steady metallic shimmers of the turbulence filling my ears. Mark spoke inaudibly to his wife from time to time, but he didn't address me again, nor did anyone else there, stunned as they shook to and fro in the belly of the machine. I found myself gazing at the window over Mark's left shoulder, focusing on the droplets of rain that slammed against the glass, each one forming for the briefest of moments before being violently whipped away by the high-velocity, unforgiving winds. I thought of the conscious entities sitting with me in that helicopter—beings that had formed only two years earlier. Two years! None of them knew it; none of them had the slightest idea of how temporary and unimportant Kali thought they were.

Then I remembered John, Haywire, and Mr. Big. Three people from the future, augmented like Kali, but mindful of from whence they'd come. So mindful, in fact, that they were willing to risk their lives to rescue mere computer programs in a sim because of their feelings of empathy for them. They were extraordinary people, post-human or not, and it was a glimmer of hope to think that somehow, compassion and empathy would still be alive in the future—at least for some.

A sudden blink of light from the window brought me out of my engrossing musings and sent a sharp jolt of surprise through my chest. I narrowed my eyes, not sure if the light had been a figment of my imagination. Then another whizzed by the window like a golden laser beam. I twisted my body around in my seat so I could see through the window over my left shoulder. The helicopter had flown out of the claustrophobic cloud cover that had been ubiquitous in my life and the lives of all the other dwellers of our sim city; it was now flying through the clear night, skirting the edge of the mountains and the sea as it raced north. I turned back to Mark's window and realized that the golden lights were the headlights of cars driving by on the highway that clung to the mountainside. We were following the shoreline.

The ride became smoother as we continued through the clear night for a few more minutes. Not long after, the helicopter turned inland, following the highway a short distance toward a small, touristy ski town I had never visited. I saw the village lights glowing softly and warmly, the town appearing like a miniaturized model from the air; it briefly occurred to me that it looked fake—then I remembered it was.

"Oh my God!" Mark suddenly shouted, his face as baffled as it was horror-stricken as he seemed to look right at me. In fact, everyone on his side of the helicopter seemed to be looking at me.

I reached up to my face to see what was the matter, checking for any sort of abnormality. Was I dematerializing into nothingness in front of them? Then I realized that it wasn't me they were looking at. From the corner of my eye, I glimpsed that the people on my side of the helicopter were all turned around, looking out of the windows on our side of the copter closest to them, mouths gaping, awe struck by what they saw.

I turned.

Our helicopter had landed on the cliff's edge of the sim—the very precipice of the end of the world.

1 1

As you well know, one cannot really fathom the abyss unless one has seen it for his or herself. It was like nothing I could have imagined. My head spun as I looked at it, trying desperately to comprehend such darkness. Such emptiness. Such nothingness.

The helicopter had flown from the city, out of the shroud of clouds, up north to the trendy ski village that had hosted a Winter Olympics, and then...*poof!* We'd flown through a small mountain pass, turned a corner, and found ourselves face to face with the end of the world.

"Uh...the world's flat?" Mark said in disbelief. "That's not supposed to be right. Is it?"

The larger door at the back of the helicopter began to open, lowering itself to form a ramp. I nearly swallowed my tongue from surprise when I saw Haywire at the bottom of the ramp, beckoning for me to join her.

"I don't know what question to ask first..." I muttered to her as I exited the helicopter in the crowd of dozens of other ghosts in the machine.

"Virtual gods, remember?" she said as she hooked her arm in mine and began to escort me to the edge of the world.

"Virtual gods have something against riding in helicopters?"

She laughed. "Well, if you had the choice between riding in your self-driving, electric car or taking, say, a horse and buggy, which would you choose?"

"You realize I have no idea what you're talking about, don't you?" I pointed out.

"Yeah," she nodded. "I know. Don't worry. Everything will make sense soon enough."

We walked to the edge. It was at once the most amazing and most terrifying thing I'd ever seen. It looked the way I'd always imagined death would look: lonely, empty, quiet, and eternal. Instinctively, I turned away from it, shuddering as I did so, and looked back at the world. I saw the warm glow of the ski village not far away, just around the bend, and saw more helicopters hovering as they came in for their landings. But mostly, I saw the faces of the people, frightened and corralled like sheep. There were hundreds of them there, but soon there would be thousands. I suddenly felt an overwhelming sense of love for them—they were the opposite of the darkness—of the emptiness—of the loneliness. They were the opposite of the chasm of black before me.

"I know it seems a bit frightening," Haywire said, a hint of sympathy in her voice, "but this is the exit. All we have to do is get these people to cross the plane, to go into the liminal space."

I turned back to her, my face painted with disbelief. "What? Are you telling me you expect them to jump off a cliff?" I reacted. "They're not lemmings, Haywire. They're *conscious*. You may have some difficulty convincing them to do that," I said, understating for effect.

"They don't have to *jump*," Haywire replied. "There's nothing that dramatic—unfortunately." She seemed slightly disappointed. "That'd be cool," she whispered under her breath, barely loud enough for me to catch it. She motioned with her hand and, out of the nothing, came forth a series of horseshoe-shaped metallic doors, each one glowing brightly, a white, ethereal light emanating from the other side. "We've learned from experience that people prefer to walk into mysterious white lights rather than hurl themselves off cliffs into darkness." She gestured to the doors, her disappointment clearly growing. "So...there are the lights." She sighed. "Damn. Jumping would be so much cooler to watch."

"We don't have time for 'cool,'" John said as he approached us. "There are many lives to save and we must be as efficient as possible."

"Ladies and gentlemen, Mr. No Fun!" Haywire announced in a half-hearted mocking, as though she were introducing John Doe for a set at Carnegie Hall.

"Are you saying the doorways are just for show?" I asked.

"Yes," John replied, expressionless.

"But...why?"

"Like I said," Haywire answered, "people like walking into white lights."

"*I'm* not particularly enthusiastic about the idea," I countered.

"That's unfortunate," John replied. "We were hoping you'd volunteer to go first."

1 2

It took me a moment to formulate a response. "Me? Why me?"

"Isn't it obvious?" John replied. "You're the only one amongst this multitude who knows what's really going on. We don't have time to try to convince the rest of them that crossing the liminal space is safe."

I turned back to the white lights. Panic gripped me. White light or not, it wasn't heaven that I saw. All I saw in there was death, and I had no desire to make the journey. "Have you ever heard of a Sonderkommando?"

"Of course," John replied, his eyes narrowing.

"Wait," Haywire said, holding up her index finger to get my attention. "I haven't."

"Sonderkommandos were Jews who worked at Nazi death camps," John informed her, all the while keeping his eyes locked on mine. "They worked for the Nazis and ran the crematoriums."

"Oh," Haywire repeated, this time understanding. "Rather dark."

"Among their ghastly duties, they were tasked with lulling the Jews who'd been selected for immediate gas chamber execution into a false sense of security," John continued. "The Sonderkommandos led them to the gas, reassuring them that they were merely going to take a shower. The gas chamber victims were the only Jews the Sonderkommandos were allowed to speak to in the camps, since the Sonderkommandos were considered *Geheimnisträger* by the guards."

"*Geheim*-what now?"

"'Bearers of secrets,'" I translated for Haywire, my eyes still locked intently on John's.

"So, you think you might be guiding these people to their deaths?" Haywire reacted, smiling.

It was clear that she found my implication absurd, but I remained silently terrified.

"I've got to admit, he's got an impressive wit," Haywire observed to John as she pointed at me with her thumb. She then gestured to the scene unfolding behind him. "I mean, the military herding people out into the night, not telling them where they're going. He made those connections quickly, and the analogy shows complex neural patterning."

"But it's deeply flawed," John replied to her before addressing me. "*You* have to be better," he said in earnest. "We can't afford to have you make mistakes in logic like this. Too many people are depending on you."

"I-I'm sorry," I said, stepping away from him and covering my eyes. "It's just...too much to take right now."

"The stress must be almost unbearable," Haywire said to John, her tone filled with obvious sympathy for me as she urged John to mirror her understanding.

"It doesn't matter," John replied tersely as he continued to stare at me, his eyes boring holes. "He has an enormous responsibility, and he must shoulder it. If he can't do that, then he doesn't belong in the real world."

I took my hand from my eyes and stared, aghast. Was John really suggesting that he would abandon me if I didn't cooperate? That he would leave me to die in a collapsing sim? If so, it called into question whether the compassion and empathy with which I'd credited them was merely another illusion in my unreal world.

"Careful, John," Haywire said quietly but firmly. "He won't understand what you mean."

"I'm right here, damn it! Stop speaking *about* me and speak to *me*!" I shouted, exasperated.

"Use your reason and logic," John insisted, ignoring my emotional outburst. "Other than the extremely superficial elements Haywire pointed out, in what ways are we like Nazis? Hm?"

I stood there, unable to reply.

"Idiots see superficial similarities between two things and conclude that they are alike. *Not you!* Our world has enough idiots! *Think!*"

I didn't understand what he meant; I'd been under the impression that everyone was augmented in the real world. There was so much I still wasn't able to grasp.

"We're not corralling Jews with the intention of throwing them in the ovens—your analogy was offensive and stupid. Use your logic! You've watched events unfold, just as we predicted they would. We have not deceived you for a moment. And what if we were? To what end? How could it possibly benefit us to enter a sim and then elaborately trick you and several thousand other people into killing themselves? If we wanted to kill you, we'd have done it already. Believe me, no elaborate ruses would be necessary."

"He's right," Haywire said to me, her tone soft but frank. "You've been through a lot, and been stressed to the brink, but if you think it through clearly, you'll realize that your fear isn't rational. You're completely safe, and all we're asking you to do is be the first person in this sim to cross the threshold into a new and better life."

I took several moments to digest their words. I stared at the white light and calculated. When I controlled my fear and thought things through, I understood that my fears were absurd. I hadn't wanted to enter the doorway because I was afraid of what was on the other side—afraid of the "undiscovered country," as the Bard called it—afraid of death. But to remain in the sim, in the illusion, to remain a ghost in the machine would be true death. It occurred to me that I wasn't really scared of death...I was scared of life. "To be or not to be," I whispered to myself.

"Yes," John responded immediately. "That *is* the question. But I don't believe that Hamlet was only pondering whether he should live or die. Rather, he was weighing whether he should live a life of purpose—a life over which he'd taken control—or whether he should simply exist, giving up control of the events around him. My dear Professor, if you wish, we shall allow you to reenter the crowd and shuffle through the exit along with them." He stepped to me and put his arm on my shoulder. "*Or*...you can take control of this situation and lead your brethren to safety. The choice is yours."

I turned once again to the huddled masses, standing with blankets over their shoulders, at least 100 post-humans dressed in military fatigues guiding them to their places in the waiting area. Most of that teeming throng were looking my way.

"I'll do it."

1 3

"I'm sure most of you know who I am," I said as confidently as I could, a microphone in my hand as I stood on a small platform that the post-humans had erected in front of the crowd. As I looked out into the growing sea of faces, now numbering in the thousands, I was cognizant that it would be my last speaking engagement. I'd dazzled crowds for years, enthralling the assembled masses with my confident, eloquent, and—as some of my detractors might have said—arrogant demonstrations of future technology. I'd enraptured crowds by showing them possibilities made real, held in the palm of my hands or worn on my wrist or over my eyes. My face was synonymous with the future—with the impossible, possible. "If you don't know who I am, I'm sure someone in the crowd will fill you in."

They laughed nervously.

I paced as I collected my thoughts. I wondered how many of these keynote speeches I'd actually given and how many of them had been memory implants. It suddenly dawned on me that my earlier career had been implanted into the memories of all of those assembled as well. "We've been through a lot together," I said, grimacing as I tried to comprehend that my life as I'd known it was over, never to return. "We've seen the world change a lot. I hope our shared experiences have built some level of trust between us. I hope you know I mean what I say. I hope you realize I'd *never* lie to you, for you mean too much to me."

At that point, I could sense their fear; if I could have stretched out my arms to shelter them all, I would have.

"I'm here to promise you that you *will* be okay. Your families will remain together. Everyone here will be safe. But to accomplish this, we have to recognize the reality." I sighed and gestured toward John and Haywire. "We've been evacuated by the authorities because there is a catastrophic danger approaching. It *will not* pass. We can't ignore it. We can't fight it, but there is an action we must take if we are to overcome it."

The fear rumbled through the crowd.

I held my hands up to soothe them and to quiet their gasps and murmurs; if I could have reached out to wipe the tears from the eyes of the mothers holding their little ones, looking on in terror, I would have. "What I ask of you will be simple. It's nothing to fear." I turned to the gateways and pointed to them. "Those, my friends, are exit points! I know they appear strange to you, and I know you're as frightened of them as I was at first, but there's no reason to be. They are a top-secret, last-resort evacuation vehicle, and they will be our salvation."

The crowd was baffled into almost complete silence.

"Evacuating the city isn't enough!" I announced, sending them into a temporary panic, but I knew they could be reeled back in. "The terrorist destruction that is coming will incinerate everything that does not escape through those gates!"

The silence returned. Now they knew the stakes.

"You will not be herded through those gates. You're not animals. Everyone who walks through the gateway will do so of his or her own freewill. The choice is yours, but to show you that there is nothing to fear," I said, nodding to the crowd, "I'll be the first one to go through." I handed the microphone to John and then stepped down from the platform and joined Haywire.

We walked to the gateway together.

"Well done, Professor," she said, sounding impressed. She looped her arm in mine. "You should have seen that from my point of view. Brad Pitt giving an inspirational speech before risking his life? Definitely doable."

"What?"

"It's a joke. Geesh. Nobody has a sense of humor."

I stepped to the foot of one of the gateways and gulped a breath of air, steeling myself. I turned back to the crowd; they were watching my every move, enraptured. I thought of the keynote I'd given a mere thirty-six hours earlier. I'd felt none of it was real then—as though I were playing a role. Now, I felt more purpose than I'd ever felt in my life. For as long as I'd lived, I'd wanted to make the future real, and now I finally had that chance. I could literally step into the future, lead all of them to a better world. I waved to the crowd and smiled confidently.

"Break on through to the other side," Haywire encouraged, smiling. "I'll see you there."

I nodded. "Looking forward to it."

I turned and entered the light.

14

WAKING UP was an experience that was denied to me. Fingers dug into my shoulder as a hand grasped me and pulled me roughly backward, out of the white light. I blinked several times, disoriented, as the world that I thought I'd left reappeared, though dramatically altered. "What the hell is going on?"

The sky was flashing, alternating between a deep indigo blue and a glowing pink; together, they blended into a dreadful purple hue, etched with strange patterns that appeared like fragments of code and small globes and sparks of light. The bizarre display was extraordinarily uncomfortable to observe and made it extremely difficult for me to regain my bearings.

All the while, Haywire held me firm with the hand that had snatched me from the light while she waved her other hand in front of me, manipulating data screens and lines of code that hovered just inches in front of my body, seemingly having been extracted from inside me. "Oh, dear God," she suddenly said, her complexion turning even whiter than normal. "John! She embedded a lynchpin program into him!"

"A wh-hat?" I stammered.

"That's impossible!" John exclaimed, addressing Haywire and ignoring me entirely again. "We would've detected it!"

"Not this one," Haywire replied. "This one was split into almost a million different fragments, too small to be detected. When he tried to exit the sim, they were automatically activated and merged. We're lucky. If it weren't for the delay, we'd all be dead."

I thrust my hand between them to get their attention. "Not another word unless it's spoken to me in the form of an explanation!" I yelled, exasperated.

Haywire grimaced. "Kali is better than us," she said with a defeated sigh. "She had hidden protections built into the sim, and now we're screwed, big time."

"What are you talking about? Why?"

"She embedded a lynchpin program into you, put it into your coding, splitting it into pieces and burying it so deep that we couldn't detect it. It means if you leave the sim, Professor, the sim turns off."

Absurdly, I held my hands up to my torso and placed my palms flat against the flesh where Haywire had been extracting the holographic coding. I suddenly felt as though I were an unwilling suicide bomber, explosives strapped and locked onto my chest. "You saved my life," I uttered.

Haywire scoffed. "Heh. Yours is the only life I didn't save, bub. If you'd exited, you would've been okay. It's the rest of us that would've been screwed."

"Haywire!" John whispered harshly, his eyes wild and threatening.

Haywire rolled her eyes. "Relax, John. He won't do it."

"Do what?" I asked.

"Run through the exit," Haywire replied. "You're not a mass murderer now, are you, Professor?"

I was aghast at the suggestion, and the expression I displayed to John demonstrated that clearly. "How dare you?"

"It's the logical move for you," John countered. "All rational beings act in their own self-interest. Running out now guarantees your survival."

"I shall take your inference that I am irrational as a compliment then."

"Let us not forget, Professor, that you implied that we might be cyber-Nazis."

"Right," I conceded. "I suppose we're even then. You're not Nazis, and I'm not a selfish bastard who'd let thousands die so that I could save myself." I turned back to Haywire. "What happens now?"

Haywire shook her head, refocusing. "The sim will purge itself."

"Purge?" I asked.

Haywire offered no answer, so I turned back to John for an explanation.

"Worse than Dante or Blake," he said.

15

"Lynchpin programs are designed to keep a principal character from exiting a sim," Haywire further elaborated. "If one is triggered, it means the principal must have been contacted by and come under the influence of hackers—that'd be us. If you've got hackers in your sim, the most efficient defense is to purge the system."

"The NPCs will turn on each other," John translated, his tone foreboding. "They'll tear one another apart in a Battle Royale until there's only one left standing—one out of millions."

"This is all in an effort to find and destroy *us*," Haywire continued.

I imagined the carnage as they described it; my imagination failed me. "Is this, uh...purge, is it happening now?"

"It would've started the moment when the lynchpin program activated," John confirmed. "It is not hyperbole to say that, at this moment, the streets of every major city in this sim are running with blood."

The image caused me to grimace involuntarily. "So what do we do? Surely all is not lost?"

Haywire and John exchanged glances with each other.

"What?" I demanded.

"There's no easy solution," Haywire replied. "We have to bide our time and continue the evacuation as planned."

I turned to the assembled masses of conscious entities, who remained corralled, huddled together, the post-human sentries who guarded them not taking action. "Then why aren't you moving them out?"

"We can't," Haywire answered. "The gates are locked."

"What?" I responded, terror gripping my simulated heart. "You mean we're trapped?"

"Yes."

"Then what do we do?"

"We have friends on the outside," Haywire replied. "Once they realize we've been cut off and the gates are closed, they'll go to work to hack their way in. Eventually, we'll get those doors open."

"In the meantime," John interjected, "we have to keep these people safe, and we need to make sure Kali remains..." John trailed off, his head tilting back with surprise, concern narrowing his eyes. "Haywire, can you reach Mr. Big?"

"Oh no," she whispered as John's alarmed expression spread to hers. "No!" she shouted after several moments of trying to establish a connection. "This is crazy! Kali's lynchpin program is more advanced than anything we've ever seen! It cut off our communication!"

"We've underestimated her, it seems," John replied, slight admiration for Kali commingling with controlled alarm in his tone.

At that moment, four of the post-humans dressed in far more advanced military garb than I'd ever seen before, joined our huddle. "Our communication has been cut off," one of them announced.

"We're aware," John replied. "Everyone must remain calm. If we panic, we'll frighten those who are in our care."

"Agreed," one of the post-humans said with a firm nod.

"First things first," John announced. "We must secure Kali's safety."

"What?" I reacted, stunned. "What makes you think *she* isn't safe? Mr. Big is with her, right?"

"Yes, along with three other post-humans, but they're also in the middle of a heavily populated urban sim that is in the throes of purging itself. NPCs do not play favorites. Right now, they're pattern recognizers with only one purpose— to destroy anything that appears human. They won't discriminate. If they find Kali, they will kill her, and if she dies, we all die.

"If this is a rescue mission, count me in," said one of the post-human soldiers as he rested his gun on his shoulder.

"I'm afraid not, my friend," John replied. "We need you and the others to remain here to guard the sims." He turned to Haywire. "Head back to the city to make sure Kali is secure, and assist Mr. Big. The professor will join you." He turned back to his friends in the military garb. "We can't currently download any assistance from the outside, so we'll have to make do with what we have here in the sim already. The professor will require means to protect himself so, gentlemen, if you'd be so kind..."

"Sure," the post-human replied as he reached with his hand and grasped at his chest, as though he were trying to pull a spiderweb from his torso. A holographic copy of his armor came free in his hand, and he handed it to John, the image suddenly solidifying into a tangible object before my eyes.

"Here you go," John said, thrusting the chest plate toward me. "Just slap it to your chest," he said, demonstrating the motion for me with his own hand.

I did as he asked, slapping the armor absurdly against my chest, only to gasp in shock as the armor opened up and suctioned onto my body, sealing me inside it. It wasn't just protection for my chest that I had acquired, however. The armor then snaked down my arms and legs, forming a full-body suit, gloves, boots and all.

"Good," John said with an approving nod. "The armor is impenetrable in the sim. If you're cornered by NPCs, they won't be able to claw or bite their way through." John turned back halfway to the post-human, his hand outstretched, and his palm flat in expectation as his eyes remained locked on mine. The post-human didn't miss a beat, copying his large firearm and placing the copy in John's open, waiting hand. John held it up for me to see. "This doesn't fire bullets. It's a pattern disruptor. Anything you shoot with it will come apart, whether it's an NPC or a solid brick wall." He placed it firmly in my hand. "Just make sure you don't accidentally shoot yourself in the foot with it."

The post-humans shared a laugh.

John turned to them briefly, but then turned back to me, his face completely humorless. "I'm serious. It would kill you."

"Okay," I replied sheepishly.

"As good as these protections and armaments are, you're far from invulnerable," John continued. "The armor will protect you against sharp objects like teeth, claws, knives—even bullets won't be able to breach it. But if you find yourself surrounded by a large enough group of NPCs, make no mistake. They *will* be able to kill you. There's nothing preventing them from crushing your windpipe or smothering you with their vast numbers."

The thought conjured an image of a nasty death in my mind; I blinked hard to make it go away. I turned to the post-humans. I was adorned in their same protective equipment, minus one important exception. "What about a helmet?" I asked. "Don't you think—"

John reached out swiftly and pulled my aug glasses from my face. Then he swiped his hand in front of a sensor on the front of the armor's large collar. A helmet instantly formed around my head, as though it were inflating, yet the parts were solid. A HUD, far more advanced than my aug glasses, flashed on. Instantly, the pattern recognizers in my suit locked onto the assembled post-humans, but they quickly unlocked, dismissing them as non-targets. "Your gun is synched with your onboard system now. If you find yourself in the company of any hostile targets, it will guide your hands and shoot."

"All you have to do is go along for the ride," said the post-human who'd so generously copied his equipment for me.

"Literally," Haywire jumped in. "John, you realize that if our communications have been cut off, then our teleportation capability will have gone along with it."

"Teleportation?" I reacted, surprised. "*That's* how you got here so fast?"

Haywire didn't reply to me directly, instead pointing her thumb at me as she commented to John, "Check out Sherlock over here."

"The trip is manageable," John replied. "Just fly him there. When you are confident that Kali is secure, you, Mr. Big, the professor, and the others need to get back here as quickly as you can. There's no telling how long it will take those on the outside to hack the gates, and you *don't* want to be left behind."

"You're staying here?" I asked.

"Yes. This is the largest pocket of conscious sims, and they'll need our protection. We're off the beaten path, and I'm not expecting trouble, but if the villagers somehow catch wind that we're here before they've finished purging themselves, we'll be in for one hell of a fight."

"But what can NPCs do to *you*?"

"Admittedly, not much," John replied, "but a large enough herd of them can be extraordinarily dangerous. I'll remain here to lead a repulse attack if necessary. Now, you two," he said to Haywire and me, "go!" With that, he turned and walked with his four companions back down the incline, toward the helpless, confused crowd.

"We're going to have to fly," Haywire said, turning and walking toward a nearby clearing through the brush.

"But the helicopters are in the opposite direction," I commented, confused as she walked away from the only mode of flight that I could see. "You're going the wrong way."

She shook her head. "I don't think so, Professor." She bent over slightly and motioned for me to join her. I cocked my head back, astonished when I realized that she wanted me to get onto her back! "Are you joking?"

"Afraid not. Look, I'm not looking forward to it either. You're going to be heavy as hell."

"Are you telling me you can fly?"

Wordlessly, she turned to me and levitated a meter in the air before quickly coming back to earth. She sighed impatiently. "Enough demonstration? Now get onboard, big fella."

I hesitantly lifted my leg up, allowing her to scoop first it, and then the other, under her arms.

"Oh damn!" she exhaled. "You're heavy! Why the hell did John do this to me? I could have done this alone!"

She lifted off and I wrapped my arms tight around her torso.

"Because he doesn't trust me," I replied. "He thinks I'll run through the gates."

1 7

Haywire and I had entered the gray abyss nearly twenty minutes earlier, and I held tight to her torso like a child as I waited for the abyss to crack and the city to reemerge. John Doe's foreboding prediction that it would be worse than the worst imaginings of Dante and Blake had me casting horrific images of flesh burning in flames and people clawing one another to death. I was expecting to witness a holocaust. What we saw emerging from the gray, through the slivers that opened in the cloud and rain, allowing us see the city, disturbed us for altogether different reasons. Indeed, the city was not burning, nor was it tearing itself apart; rather, it was at a perfect standstill.

"What the hell is going on?" Haywire asked as we flew over the bridge and witnessed it devoid of traffic. She skimmed over the treetops in the park, and the downtown core materialized from out of the clouds. The glow of the city lights was peaceful, yet somehow cold and unwelcoming, as though they were lights in a painting on the wall in a frozen room. "Where is everybody?"

Almost the instant she asked, I noticed a woman standing on the sidewalk, her body so rigid and her spine so straight that I could easily have mistaken her for a street lamp or mailbox, as she was just as fixed in place. She stared straight ahead at the wall of the building across the street from her. In the building, I noticed something even more disturbing. "Haywire, look at the windows," I said, pointing to the building.

"Oh my God," Haywire reacted, astonished.

The windows of the building, along with the windows of the other high-rises in the downtown core, were dotted with the faces of people standing and staring straight forward, out into the night. "What are they waiting for? Why aren't they purging the sim?"

"You said Kali had outsmarted you with her undetectable lynchpin program. Perhaps delaying or avoiding a purge is another example of her outthinking your post-human organization."

"But why?" Haywire replied as we banked to the left and headed north, across the water and toward my penthouse. "The point of lynchpin programs is to serve as protection against hacktivists. They initiate purges so the hackers can be weeded out and eliminated. If she doesn't purge the sim, she has nothing. No defense whatsoever."

"That's only assuming that Kali is as limited as the other targets of your hacking activities were. The complex encryption in her lynchpin program has already established that this is not the case. We should be on our guard. Kali must be thinking outside the box."

"Well, well. Look at you," Haywire replied condescendingly over her shoulder as we neared my penthouse. "Figuring stuff out. You're a quick study, aren't ya?"

"I only hope that I represent my primitive, un-enhanced primate brethren well," I replied, tiring of the post-human tendency to underestimate me.

"Oh, and he's getting funny too! You're full of surprises tonight."

We set down on my balcony, and Haywire immediately shrugged me off her back, seemingly relieved to dispatch her burden. She stretched as though her back had stiffened.

"Isn't your body only an avatar?" I noted.

She glared at me as she rubbed her shoulder. "The avatars simulate reality—maybe a little *too* well sometimes. And for the record, your muscle mass is meant to be devoured by women's eyes, not carried on their backs."

I nodded. "My apologies."

"Mr. Big?" Haywire called out into the penthouse. The wet, cold wind blew the curtains ominously as Haywire entered the darkened living space in search of her companions. When no answer was returned, I immediately became alarmed, fear causing me to grasp my gun with both hands, holding it in front of me as I stepped slowly through the doorway. "Haywire, something's wrong."

"Yeah, I'm thinking that too," she whispered as she stood outside my bedroom door, waiting for me to join her. She looked at my gun. "Raise your weapon. Get ready to fight."

18

Haywire placed the side of her hand against the bedroom door and began to push it open. For the second time that night, I found myself on the verge of praying that Kali would be there, asleep in the bed—and for the second time, that prayer would go unanswered.

"Oh no," Haywire whispered.

"Maybe they moved her to a more secure location," I suggested.

"No. They didn't," Haywire replied, her shoulders slumping as she stepped forward, moving toward something I couldn't see on the ground in front of my bed.

I craned my neck to peer past the door for a better view. I wasn't prepared for what I saw.

Body parts. Blood. Agony.

"What the hell happened?" Haywire asked as she took Mr. Big's armless, legless, eyeless body into her arms, cradling him against her.

"She was never asleep," Mr. Big gasped painfully, his mouth filling with blood that he had to spit away every few seconds. "She...took us by surprise. We couldn't even fight back...ripped everyone apart...only left me alive to give you a message."

"What?" Haywire asked, her face twisted in torment as she rocked her comrade in a wasted attempt to be soothing; nothing could soothe pain like that.

I scanned the room. There were arms, legs, torsos, and enough blood to coat the entire floor crimson. I shifted slightly and kicked something accidentally. I looked down, realizing it was someone's face. It skidded to a halt near Haywire, but she didn't notice the grotesque interruption, her attention riveted to Mr. Big.

"She said, 'where the mind's acutest reasoning is joined to evil will and evil power...there human beings can't defend themselves.'"

Haywire's face was aghast. "What the hell is that—"

"She's quoting Dante's *Inferno*," I said.

Haywire's expression remained the same. "Why? What the hell for?"

I shook my head.

"You've got to kill me!" Mr. Big suddenly shouted, snapping Haywire's attention back to him.

"I won't do that and you know it," Haywire immediately replied, dismissing the request.

"You *have* to!" Mr. Big's voice was corrupted by the pain to the point that the high, desperate pitch he reached was inhuman. "I'm in agony!"

"Listen to me! You've still got your appendages in the real world. She cauterized the wounds. You *can* hold out and we *can* get you out of this!"

"There's no getting out of this!" Mr. Big screamed. "We're in her head, damn it! She's awake, and we're in her head! There's no escaping this! We're all going to die—every single one of us!" The big man writhed in pain; it sounded as though he wanted to shed tears, but a cursory glance of the size of the holes where his eyes had been ripped from his skull was enough to confirm that he had no tear ducts. Dried tears of blood, however, streaked his cheeks.

"So what? You're just going to die?" Haywire retorted. "Unacceptable!"

"You can put my back-up mind file into my body," Mr. Big replied, pleadingly, negotiating for his own death.

Haywire shook her head.

He couldn't have seen her refusal, but somehow he seemed to sense it. "Yes you can. You can! I backed it up right before we hacked Kali's sim!"

"You can back up your brains?" I asked, astonished.

Haywire ignored me and continued to address the fallen. "It's too risky. We have to unlock the gates first."

Mr. Big's only response was a long, forlorn moan. I couldn't fathom the torment he was enduring. He was willing to risk ending his real life to end the pain in the sim.

Suddenly, I felt a low vibration in the soles of my boots. I raised my weapon and stepped back quickly to the door of the room and peered out into the hallway. The vibration—whatever it was—was growing.

"What is it?" Haywire called to me, sensing it as well.

"I don't know," I replied as the vibrations grew, sounding more and more like a coming stampede of wild horses as it neared. "But I think we should get out of here immed—"

Before I could finish my suggestion, my right arm yanked me around and forced me to take aim at an incensed man in a blue dress shirt and khaki pants as he sprinted from the elevator toward me. The pattern disruptor gun fired without me pulling the trigger, a golden jet of particles hitting him in the chest and ripping him apart into nothing but waves of distortion, like the air above a hot asphalt road on a sunny July day. Before I could even react, the gun fired twice more at two more NPCs, the two barely able to make it out of the elevator before the gun cut them down.

"Nice shooting, Tex," Haywire commented as she joined me outside the bedroom door.

"I didn't—"

"Autopilot, I know," Haywire replied, cutting me off. The sound of the menacing stampede was swelling. "Let's get the hell outta here."

We turned back to the bedroom to retrieve what was left of Mr. Big, only to stop in our tracks as a wave of NPCs reached the railing of my balcony. They vaulted over it preternaturally in leaps that would put Olympic gymnasts to shame, and rushed toward us like river rapids about to sweep us away.

The computer in my suit identified targets in rapid succession, aiming and firing several times a second, nearly ripping my shoulder out of its socket as it locked on, dispatched, and then quickly found the next most threatening NPC. Even with the speed of the futuristic targeting software guiding the hardware in the suit and gun, I still couldn't shoot fast enough to stop the tide of enemies from overwhelming us.

Luckily, Haywire had it covered. She used her left leg to kick me in the ribs with enough force to knock me out of her way, somehow managing to avoid injuring me. She then thrust her arms forward, palms out, as though she were trying to move an invisible truck out of her way. Just as Kali had done to me in the same hallway, Haywire was able to force the NPCs backward, ramming what must have been fifty of them out to the balcony and beyond, sending each one tumbling violently over the railing.

"Impressive," I commented.

She watched as, immediately, the next wave of NPCs, apparently oblivious to the fate of their predecessors, launched themselves over the railing and into the apartment. Again, she sent her invisible force-field toward them, slamming them all backwards, sending their bodies twirling out into the rain-drenched night, spiraling to their deaths, only to collide with the pavement far below. Then she turned to me and grabbed me by my arm, thrusting me back into my bedroom before shutting the door with one hand and then gesturing with the other, seemingly summoning every inanimate object in the room to her and then piling them up as a barricade. "That'll only hold 'em for seconds at most. We have to get out of here."

She strode to Mr. Big, grabbing him by the collar of his shirt and dragging him to the window. Then she turned back to me, looking at me impatiently as I stood, dumbfounded, next to the bedroom door. "Why are you just standing there? My Jedi mind tricks can't hold them back forever. We've got to fly out of here before—"

Before she could finish her sentence, the bedroom window smashed, and the first NPC's bloodied fingers grasped desperately toward her. She turned and used her force-field power once again, sending the NPC tumbling out into the night, but another three instantly took its place. She sent them off the edge as well, but they were quickly replaced by five more. "This is bad!" she shouted. "I can't get on top of them, and we need to get the hell out of here— like yesterday!"

On my right side, the door Haywire had barricaded with the heavy oak dresser, my bed, the twin nightstands, the entire contents of my walk-in closet, and the body parts of the deceased post-humans was undulating from the force of the NPCs as they piled their bodies against it. Not only were they mere seconds from breaking down the door, but it appeared they were mere seconds from bringing down the entire wall of the bedroom. I stepped away from the door, my head swiveling from the door to the window, where Haywire continued to send NPCs to their ultimate demises. There appeared to be no escape.

Then I remembered something John Doe had said. I raised my weapon again, this time pointing straight up at the ceiling, and I fired. Just as John had related, the section of the ceiling I'd shot disappeared, leaving a hole that was more than a meter deep in the concrete. I surmised that the rooftop couldn't be much further. I shot twice more, the golden pattern dematerializing the concrete, erasing it form the sim. When the rain began pouring into the room, I knew my efforts were not wasted.

"Haywire! C'mon! I made us an exit!"

She looked over her shoulder at me briefly, then up at the hole I'd shot into the ceiling. "Can we fit through there? It looks narrow!"

I shot twice more. "I widened it. We'll be okay!"

"What about Mr. Big? We can't leave without him, but the second I leave this window, NPCs are going to pour into the room!"

I ran to Mr. Big and grabbed him as securely as I could, hooking my hand into the waist of his pants. "I got him!"

"Leave me..." Mr. Big whimpered.

Haywire ignored his protest. "Brace yourself!" she shouted as she sent another force blast out toward the intruding NPCs. Then she turned, hooked her arm under mine, and flew toward the hole in the ceiling. I fired one last pattern disruptor shot at the first NPC who made it into the room, but before I could fire another, we'd already entered the narrow hole, Haywire dragging me as I dragged Mr. Big. We were making our way through three and a half meters of concrete, but before we could escape, an NPC had already, uncannily, reached Mr. Big. The remnant of the gigantic man was wrenched out of my arm in a fraction of a second, so unceremoniously that I was still in shock as we cleared the rooftop. A second after that, the NPCs began erupting like a geyser from the hole I'd created, spouting up, using each other's bodies like ladders to climb as they preternaturally leapt and clawed at us, more than one of them coming quite close before falling back to the rooftop.

"Where'd he go?" Haywire screamed to me.

"I lost him," I replied, fixing my eyes on the atrocious spectacle that shrank away behind us, the entire building swarmed by NPCs like bees on a honeycomb, covering every inch of the building exterior until the walls themselves seemed to move.

As I watched the spectacle, Mr. Big's words echoed in my head: *"We're all going to die—every single one of us."*

20

"What do you mean, you *lost* him?" Haywire shouted, shrugging me off of her back a little too early, forcing me to roll painfully across the wet gravel of the rooftop of the high-rise she'd chosen as a landing pad in the downtown core. She set down and thundered toward me, then grabbed me by the front of my armor and shook me angrily as she followed up icily, "How do you just *lose* a human being?"

"I held on as tight as a I could," I replied in protest. "The NPC...ripped him from my grasp. I didn't even feel a tug...I just had him one moment and then the next..."

Her lip curled up in disgust before she thrust me back down to the gravel. "We have to go back for him."

"That's completely irrational," I replied as I sprang back to my feet. "You're letting your emotions get the best of you."

Haywire's eyes grew wild. "Yeah. I am," she said, nodding as she stepped toward me again, her posture threatening. "Where's *your* emotion?"

"I'm feeling very emotional," I retorted, "but I am not letting it stop me from being analytical. Mr. Big was dead by the time we left the building. There's no one back there to save."

Haywire shook her head, the resentment in her eyes burning holes through me. "He was dead the moment I trusted his fate to *you*."

"I-I'm sorry. I really tried."

Haywire kept her resentful glare locked on me for several moments more before finally turning away with a disgusted snarl. She marched to the ledge of the building. "If you didn't have the lynchpin, I'd return the favor and leave *you* here to die."

"Where are you planning to go?"

She snapped her head around as though it was the stupidest question she'd ever heard. "Where do you think?"

"If you're planning to head back to the gates, I'm afraid that's no longer an option."

"What?"

"Kali's awake," I replied. "The gates north of the city are the first place she'll go in search of me. For all we know, she's already there."

"That's precisely why we need to get there immediately. John and the others need our help."

"It's exceedingly unlikely that the gates are even still there."

Haywire's mouth opened, aghast. "You cold son-of-a-bitch."

"I'm speaking the truth, am I not?" I replied. "Kali can manipulate the physical world in her sim on a scale that goes far beyond what even you and the other post-humans can achieve, correct? What makes you think the post-humans could possibly have resisted her? She would have caught them by surprise, just as she did Mr. Big and the others at my condo. I'm sorry, Haywire, but it is almost a certainty that John is already dead."

"*Almost*! That's the point!" Haywire shouted in reply. "We don't know for sure! That's why we have to go!"

"And *almost* certainly die?"

"I'm not basing my decision on math, you idiot! I'm not basing my decisions on probabilities!" she screamed at me. "No wonder you can't make a woman happy. You think like a computer!" She stepped back to the ledge before turning back to me. "This is your last chance, Professor. Are you coming with me or not?"

"Please don't be irrational," I replied. "*Think.*"

She shook her head, her expression now one of disgust mixed with bitter disappointment. "I thought you were starting to understand." She stepped off the ledge and began to fly away, but just before she disappeared into the driving rain and thick dark clouds, my HUD flashed on, an image of smoldering carnage filling the screen.

"Haywire?" John's voice spoke. It sounded as though he were in tears, as if the effort to speak was nearly too much. "Haywire, can you see what's happened?"

Haywire had frozen in the air, her back turned to me as the message clearly reached her too, stunning her still. The image we saw was one of devastation, the gates destroyed, the white light devoured by darkness, the black abyss at the end of the world appearing colder and more hopeless than ever before. "I see," she said.

The point of view panned to the right, taking in the sickening sight of thousands of charred bodies, NPCs frantically ripping and shredding through the still-smoldering corpses like frenzied animals orgiastically devouring their prey. "Haywire," John spoke again. "Do you see?" he repeated.

"Yes, John. I see."

The point of view changed again, panning around to show John on his knees, his eye sockets empty, a dozen streaks of blood running from the fresh wounds, raked down his cheeks. "That's good. That's good," John spoke.

Kali stepped into frame behind him, grinning as she placed her hand on John's shoulder. "As you *can* see, your friend can no longer see *anything.*"

21

As soon as Haywire and I saw Kali's visage, we knew we were finished. Kali had allowed John that one last grim communication for no other reason than to trace the signal and locate us so she could teleport to our location. From the moment that the shock of this realization registered, events unfolded according to pure, animal instincts. Haywire spun in the air and thrust forward toward me, her arms outstretched. I holstered my gun and held my arms out, ready to catch her and grab on for the ride. Unfortunately, as quickly as Haywire reacted, Kali was quicker on the draw, her teleportation instantaneous. She appeared out of nothing, only one meter to my right, her bare feet hovering just inches above the sharp gravel of the rooftop, her red dress wet from the rain, yet still billowing in the wind, her wet, tangled hair doing likewise. I had only enough time to turn my head to her and see her enraged, glowing LED eyes as her hands grasped for me, contorted into claws as she moved in. Her appearance matched what she truly was: the devil—the Satan of the sim she'd created. My heart slammed against the wall of my chest as the fright paralyzed me.

As her fingers contacted my armor, she was suddenly ricocheted away, far into the distance by a powerful force blast from Haywire. It was a trick that would only work once, but Haywire had caught the self-proclaimed god off guard. That bought us just enough time for Haywire to reach out, scoop me onto her back, then dip down over the ledge of the building, careening into the dark night.

"Choose an erratic path! Our only chance is to lose her in the cloud cover!" I shouted.

Haywire turned sharply to the right, nearly throwing me off of her back in the process. Then she turned left and headed down a narrow alley, where we blasted through the brick and mortar canyon. It seemed, for the briefest of moments, as though we might elude Kali, but then she turned the world against us.

Her first move was to strip us of our cover. The thick, dark, rain-filled clouds that blanketed the city evaporated in a second. The same sky we'd left behind at the gates returned: the alternating red and blue, the circuitry patterning, and the globes of light falling like soft snow, all there once again. "Stay low. We just lost our cover!"

Haywire obeyed, dropping down until we were skimming the city streets. "We have to get out of the open!"

I struggled to turn my head and crane my neck so I could see behind us. Horrified, I saw the city's structure seemingly coming to life, the NPCs flooding the streets and alleyways just as they had done in my penthouse, only on a far grander and more terrifying scale. They had spotted us, and the furious river of simulated people was rushing toward us, moving so supernaturally fast that they were actually gaining. "The NPCs have eyes on us!" I screamed.

"That means Kali has eyes on us too! She'll teleport!" Haywire made the decision to try evading the city's collective gaze by turning sharply once again and careening toward a glass office building that seemed to take up the entire city block upon which it had been erected. We smashed through the glass on the second floor, then turned sharply again down a hallway and toward the center of the building. "Let's see if we can come out the other side without anyone seeing us!"

Her plan, though rash and with little chance of succeeding, did work for a brief moment, as it allowed us to escape from the ubiquitous eyes of the NPCs. I was about to speak to her, to suggest that we try to exit through the basement, hoping there might be a way to access the sewers; I was sure there was no way an above-ground exit would facilitate our escape. Before the words could escape my lips, however, the building shifted, and the wall to our right suddenly came at us, slamming against our bodies so hard that there was no way I could continue to hold on to my ride.

The lights flickered off and I fell, sliding against the floor that was quickly rotating as the building seemed to turn on its side. Concrete dust, chunks of plaster, water from burst pipes, and an untold amount of office supplies and furniture slid down the hallway with me in an avalanche of chaos in the darkness. "Night vision!" I shouted, hopeful that the computer systems in my armored suit were equipped with the voice-activated feature. Luckily, they were, and the night vision flicked on, illuminating the scene. I was quickly sliding toward the wall that was now the floor of the building, in danger of being buried by the debris that was rapidly coming down behind me. Seeing the door to an office quickly approaching, I reached out to snag the door frame before slamming my body against the door as hard as I could. It opened and I was able to pull myself up and to use the office as a ledge as I watched the contents of the second floor of the building rush by me.

Haywire, unfortunately, was nowhere to be seen.

"Haywire?" I called out.

"Is that you, Professor?" John Doe asked, his voice pained to the point of being pathetic.

"I'm in a bit of a situation at the moment," I replied. "Kali is tracing our calls. You realize that, don't you?"

"I do. I'm sorry," John Doe replied. "I'm about to die. I can't see. But I know the NPCs can see me and that they'll kill me soon. I can't defend against them forever. Eventually, one of them will get past my force blasts...sneak behind me and sink its teeth into me. I am not facing a pleasant death, my friend. Perhaps I should consider myself lucky for not being able to see it."

"I wish I could help you," I replied as I continued to scan the hallway for Haywire. The building continued its rotation. From what I could ascertain, it appeared that Kali had removed the entire structure from its moorings and was spinning it for reasons that I didn't yet understand. The sound of the building groaning and the walls and support structures snapping and exploding under the stress was nearly deafening.

"*You're* the key," John said. "She wants the lynchpin so she can escape the sim—so she can wake up."

"I'm aware," I replied as a particularly loud grinding from behind me caused me to turn. The window to the office was sealing, the brick and mortar nearly liquefying as the walls seemed to come to life, closing off every exit. It became clear to me that Kali was turning the building into a prison. When she'd closed off all escape routes, she'd start hunting us. I knew our time was short.

"You can't let her escape," John urged. "There are other conscious entities in the sim. We hadn't yet located everyone. Even though she destroyed the largest gates, there are gates all over the sim, in every corner of the world. There are still lives that you can save. They're depending on you—whether they realize it or not."

"You have my word, John," I replied as I struggled to reenter the hallway, the building having nearly rotated a full 360 degrees, and the passageway becoming briefly traversable once again. "I'll do all I can." First, however, I had to find Haywire. As she wasn't responding to John's communiqué, it was clear that she was either unconscious or dead. I hadn't seen her fall, so I had to assume she'd been knocked into one of the offices. I had to search each one until I found her.

"I'm sorry I opened communication with you," John said, sniveling. "The torture, Professor...I-I can't describe it. She choked me unconscious. She gouged out my eyes. I couldn't resist her."

"I understand," I replied, truly sympathetic, yet unable to focus on the heroic man's dying words. I'd searched three offices so far. There were more than a dozen left in the hallway, but the building continued its rotation, the floor inching toward a ninety-degree incline that would be impossible for me to climb. I had to find Haywire before then.

"You have to understand, Professor, under torture, it *isn't you* anymore. I would never give up a comrade under normal circumstances. I'd never give anyone up. But when subjected to pain like that...it simply wasn't me. It wasn't me who contacted you! Do you understand, Professor?"

"I do," I replied, having little time to absorb his heartfelt apology—the last one he would speak in his life. I had been sprinting, but the floor was at almost a seventy-degree angle. I fell to my hands and knees to crawl to the next doorway. It would likely be the last one I could reach.

"It's so odd to die," John spoke, his tone suddenly reflective and calm. "To be erased. I'm in my last moments of existence. But I can't imagine not existing. Can you?"

I grasped the last doorframe and held on tight as the hallway once again reached a ninety-degree angle. I was dangling several meters above what would be the bottom of a fatal fall. I removed my gun from its holster and fired at the door, causing it to dematerialize. I then used all of my strength to do a reverse pull-up and climb into the room.

"To live is everything, Professor. Death is unacceptable." He suddenly screamed. "My death is unacceptable! Do you understand?"

I sighed as I saw Haywire's crumpled body in the office, gently rolling as the room continued to slowly rotate. There was an office chair next to her, along with a myriad of office supplies. I hopped down from the doorframe and landed next to her before addressing John one last time. "I understand, John."

"You must fight for every last life in this world, Professor. Yours and every last one."

Before I could respond, I heard John Doe scream out in terror. I flipped open the visual of his communication on my HUD just in time to witness multiple NPCs descending on top of the man like lions on an African gazelle, biting and ripping his flesh apart. It was the point of view of death. I flipped off the screen.

"Haywire? Can you hear me?" I spoke gently as I moved her face from side to side.

Her eyes fluttered open, but quickly shut tight in reaction to her pain.

"Holy...damn it! My shoulder! I think I broke something!" she finally said.

"Can you see?" I asked her.

She nodded, the motion clearly causing her severe discomfort. "I can see. My night vision activates automatically in low light. What the hell is going on?"

"Kali is doing some drastic remodeling to the building. She's sealing all of the exits."

"We're lucky," Haywire replied between pained groans. "If you didn't have the lynchpin, she'd just pancake us in here and be done with it. Trying to take you alive is forcing her to get fancy."

"I hadn't thought of us as particularly lucky at the moment," I replied.

"At least we're still alive."

"The glass is half full?" I mused.

Haywire's eyes immediately fell on my gun. "You need to make us a new exit. You can double your firepower, you know."

"How?" I asked quizzically, my eyes narrowed.

She held out her hand for my gun. I handed it to her, and she slapped her other palm against it. When her other hand came away, it held a gun too. "We can't download from outside the sim," she said, "but we can copy existing files." She handed me the guns. "Now you have all the weapons you need. It's time to get the hell out of here...before it's too late."

I nodded. "Will you be able to support my weight?"

"Not really, but I have no choice. Just hold on to me and keep firing straight ahead until we're out."

"Okay," I replied. "I suggest we head down."

"Sounds good," she answered. "Grab on."

I reached around her broken body and held on, having no choice but to squeeze my elbows together against her sides, inadvertently causing her to wheeze and groan again.

"Let's do it," she whispered, barely able to speak. "I'm gonna pass out if we wait any longer."

"Okay." I aimed at the wall at the bottom of the room upon which Haywire's back was pressed. "Here we go." I fired.

The wall disappeared in the same fashion as everything else I had fired at had, dematerializing into a brief pattern of golden dust before evaporating, as though erased. We dropped down into the next door office and I squeezed the triggers again, removing yet another wall. I began squeezing the triggers in rapid succession as we entered a free fall that quickly reached terminal velocity. Haywire remained below me, my torso pressed to her back, but she couldn't hold on to me, as the pain from her injuries was far too much.

I holstered one of my guns when I realized that simply squeezing my elbows against her wouldn't be enough when we reached the bottom and she had to shift direction. I wrapped my arm around her as firmly as I could, hopeful that she hadn't lost consciousness already. I fired for the last time, and the street suddenly became visible, not far below the building. Haywire would need to turn sharply to take us out of the free fall the moment we escaped the building; otherwise we'd slam into the pavement, instantly killing us both.

"Here we go! Are you ready?" I shouted.

Haywire didn't respond.

22

Thankfully, Haywire was awake after all, and her trajectory shifted dramatically as she pulled us out of our free fall the moment we exited the building, her belly coming within inches of scraping against the asphalt of the street we precariously skimmed. Debris from the unmoored building rained down around us; dust, glass, and concrete chunks pelting us before Haywire used her ability to manipulate the sim to cause the cover of a sewer opening to jettison itself into the air. In a maneuver that seemed suicidal to me, she took us both down into the hole at far too fast a speed, driving us recklessly into the darkness before slowing only an instant before we splashed into the putrid sewer water. The manhole cover dropped into place behind us, plunging us both into absolute darkness again, but my night vision immediately kicked back in.

"Haywire!" I shouted when I saw that she was completely submerged in the waist-deep sewage. I reached into the disgusting ooze and pulled her out, noticing that her face was contorted into an expression of utter agony. When she was clear of the water, she opened her mouth wide in an attempt to breathe, but it didn't appear that she was able to take anything into her lungs. "Your ribs are likely fractured," I said. I propped her back against the wall and tried my best to support her weight with my arms. "Stay calm and just try to take small breaths."

She nodded, closed her eyes, relaxed her grip on my arm, and managed to breathe a short, shallow breath. As soon as she inhaled, her face immediately contorted, especially her nose, which wrinkled up at the foul stench. "Oh God. That's awful!" She reached her palm up to my helmet and pulled at it like it were a spiderweb, just as John had done when copying my armor, then came away holding her own copy, which she quickly slipped over her head. "Much better."

"We have to get out of here. If any of the NPCs or traffic cameras saw us slip out of the building, Kali knows we're down here."

"I doubt it. All that debris would've covered our escape."

"Still, let's be on the safe side," I tried to help Haywire up onto the concrete ledge that ran the length of the tunnels.

She groaned. "Stop it! Hands off, Professor, before you kill me!"

"We can't just stay here," I said, motioning around at the dripping, stinky, mildewed walls. "This isn't a location conducive to recuperation and healing. If we stay here, we'll get weaker and die."

She paused as she took in another labored breath. "We won't. You can carry me, but you need to be stronger."

"Are you asking me to hit the gym and come back later?"

She shook her head. "I can't believe it. Another attempt at humor. You suck at it. No, I'm asking you to activate the exoskeleton in your armor."

Although she couldn't see my face as it remained shielded by my helmet and visor, if she could have seen it, she would have seen my mouth open in astonishment. "What? There's an *exoskeleton* in the armor? Why didn't you tell me? That would've come in handy back there!"

"If you'd activated it before I flew you, you would've crushed me in your arms. The suit is extremely powerful. Once you activate it, you'll be able to lift a car with the same ease you could lift a pad of paper. I didn't want you to juice me like a lemon."

"How do I turn it on?" I said, sighing as I let her oversight go, accepting her unsatisfying explanation. I was desperate to get out of that sewer.

"Just call up the feature. It's voice commanded."

"Exoskeleton on," I said. An icon appeared on my HUD asking me to confirm the command. "Yes," I said.

"Okay, *now* you can lift me," Haywire said weakly. "It'll be nice to be treated like a lady for once, instead of having to carry your big ass around."

I shrugged before bending my knees and scooping my arms under her, lifting her up, cradling her body as though she were an infant. It was a marvelous feeling. I couldn't exactly describe it as lifting her with ease, as that would've seemed like taking too much credit. I was carrying her only in the sense that one carries a passenger in their car. Indeed, it was the exoskeleton that was doing 100 percent of the work.

"That's better," Haywire said. "You can keep me stable this way and transport me."

"Now what?" I asked.

"The legs are powerful enough that you could leap a five-story building, if you want. Getting us onto this ledge shouldn't be an issue."

I nodded. "Okay. Here goes nothing." I leapt up into the air, trying not to put too much power behind it, lest I slam us both into the ceiling, possibly killing us both in the process. The leap was pathetic at best. I jumped straight into the air, just high enough to escape the water, then immediately came right back down, splashing into the filth.

Haywire called out in agony, tilting her head back as the pain shot through her. After the worst waves of it rolled by, she slapped me hard in the arm. "You idiot!"

"Sorry. This is new for me." I tried the leap again, this time guessing the right amount of force to use. We came down gently on the ledge. It was a small victory, but it still elicited a smile from me.

Without so much as a word of thanks or congratulation, Haywire said, "We need to find a place to lie low."

"Agreed." I stepped forward, getting used to the feel of the exoskeleton almost immediately. The device was remarkable, and I instantly felt superhuman. When I made it to an intersection in the tunnels, I easily leapt from one ledge to another, all the while keeping Haywire stable enough that her pained groans were mostly stifled. "Perhaps we should copy my armor so you can wear one of these suits as well? That way I wouldn't have to carry you."

"It wouldn't do any good," Haywire replied, struggling to get the words past her quivering lips. "Even with an exoskeleton, I can barely stand. Talking is almost as bad. Shut up and find us a place to hole up."

It was quickly becoming apparent that my Brad Pitt-in-*Troy* charm had worn off. I marched and leapt through the darkness, looking for some form of exit. I surmised that there had to be an access door somewhere. After several minutes of trudging, over the course of which I must have covered at least a few city blocks, I appeared to be no closer; much to my dismay, everything looked the same. I paused and opened my HUD with a voice command. "Web search."

"What are you doing? Don't go online!" Haywire urged. "She can trace it."

"Don't worry, I can't. No signal down here." I bent down and gently put Haywire down on the ledge.

"What do you mean? I'm serious, Professor. The second you go online, she'll teleport here and rip me to shreds."

"I have some experience with these things. I'll be encrypting the signal. She won't be able to follow the trail." I retrieved my gun and pointed it straight up, squeezing the trigger and de-patterning a small hole so that a Wi-Fi signal could seep through. I hid my location before initiating my Web browser, an old hacker's trick, and then searched for maps of the city's underground labyrinth. I surmised that I should be able to find a place where the sewer system and the underground subway line would nearly intersect. I found a suitable target location and then downloaded the directions before going offline. "Got it."

I picked Haywire back up and ran toward the near-junction as quickly as I could. It was only three blocks away, and we made it there in only a few minutes. When I arrived, I set her down partially, letting her legs rest on the ground while I used my other arm to prop her up. She groaned again.

Next, I retrieved my gun and made my own access to the subway tunnel, instantly boring a hole in the ancient-looking, brick wall. I replaced the gun, picked my passenger up again, and marched through.

On the other side, I slid down the slight curvature of the tubular subway tunnel, right down to the tracks. Across the way, I saw a door marked, "MAINTENANCE." I leapt across the ravine and landed right on the doorstep, then kicked slightly with my right leg. I had no trouble cracking the locked door open on the first try. "Home sweet home...at least for a little while." I reached up and grabbed the string that hung from the lightbulb in the middle of the room, the only means of illumination.

"I don't see what's so sweet about it," Haywire replied. The maintenance room was small and packed with tools and cleaning supplies. It smelled of dust, mildew, and rat droppings.

"Ugh," Haywire reacted as a rat the size of a Yorkshire Terrier scurried behind an industrial vacuum cleaner. "Great choice, Professor."

"It's a fixer upper, I'll admit," I replied as I set her down against the wall, forcing her to splay her legs out in the only part of the room clear enough to do so. "But you have to admit, nobody's going to be looking for us in here." I grabbed my gun once again and stepped around the vacuum cleaner, spotting the giant rat as it tried to hide, unable to do so with its enormous rump too large to squeeze under the vacuum bag. A moment later, I made it disappear.

"Nice. How do you know that wasn't conscious?" Haywire replied.

I paused for a moment, confused.

She waved her hand in front of her helmet, and it removed itself from her head, folding back into a collar that she easily removed. Her lips sported a sideways grin. "I'm kidding, of course. Geesh. You are horrible with humor."

I nodded. "Apparently. Now, let's get you fixed up, shall we?"

23

"What in the hell do you think you are doing?" Haywire complained, perturbed as I placed my palm flat against the middle of her chest, just above her breasts.

"Does that hurt?"

"Yes. So what? You're a doctor now?"

"I downloaded a step-by-step tutorial for examining for broken ribs while I was online."

She placed her hand on my wrist and tried to pull my arm away. The exoskeleton made that impossible, unless she used a force blast, but I acquiesced and removed my hand for her. "Thank you, Dr. Creepy Touch, but I can do a diagnostic of my avatar on my own, please and thanks. Now back off before I'm not the only one down here who needs a diagnostic."

"Oh," I replied. "Okay. I'll standby."

"Yeah."

Haywire shut her eyes, the dark eyeliner having smeared into the echo of tears shed from the pain. Almost instantly, translucent screens appeared in front of her, the holograms hovering in her field of vision. She opened her eyes and read. "Fractured two ribs. Fractured my scapula. Awesome."

"Can you fix it?" I asked.

"Fix it? Like heal myself with my mind?"

"Yes. Of course. You can manipulate the physical world. I assume you can manipulate your body as well."

"Levitating a manhole cover is one thing," Haywire replied, "that's just brute force stuff. But healing fractures in a bone requires precision control."

I narrowed my eyes. "I don't understand. Why wouldn't post-humans give themselves the ability to heal their injured avatars instantly?" It seemed to me that this would be a relatively easy feature to incorporate in their avatars. I was perplexed by how they could have made such an oversight.

Haywire shook her head. "This is *Kali's* sim. There are rules. We can bend them, but only Kali can break them."

Her answer further perplexed me. "Why?"

"It's a little beyond your pay grade, Professor. Just trust me, okay?"

"Try me."

"No," she replied, annoyed. She winced as she tried to take a deep breath. "Look, I *can* heal faster than a normal person. It would take a biologically non-enhanced human six weeks to recover from this with proper medical treatment, but I can localize my immune system's response to maximize healing time. In seventy-two hours, I'll be as good as new, but as for having the ability to snap my magic post-human fingers and weave bone fibers together in an instant? No. Sorry."

"But you have this ability in the physical world, do you not?"

She eyed me for a moment, as though sizing me up. "Sure," she replied, looking down as she did so, as though she didn't want to meet my gaze—or perhaps it was that she couldn't bare to see her own reflection in my visor while she lied.

"What year is it in the real world?" I inquired.

Haywire reached out with her right arm and put her hand firmly on my shoulder. "*I am in agony,*" she said emphatically. "You *have* to get me something for the pain."

"Are you suggesting I go up to street level to look for a local pharmacy?" I reacted in surprise. "I'd be detected immediately. There are cameras—"

"Everywhere, I know," Haywire cut me off. "Your suit has a built-in camouflage feature. It won't make you invisible in the sim—it isn't that sophisticated, unfortunately. Fooling the image on a digital camera feed, however, isn't all that difficult. The suit detects the cameras in the surrounding area and then hacks into their feeds, replacing the pixels that would usually display your image with clone-stamped pixels from the surroundings. You'll look like a distortion at most. A wobble. It won't trigger any pattern-recognizer security programs."

I remained silent for a moment. Something didn't feel right. My armor, conveniently—too conveniently—appeared to have the needed feature for me to overcome every obstacle. "Okay. I'll get you some painkillers." I stood up to leave.

"And a sling. I'll need a sling for my shoulder."

"There's a pharmacy almost right above us," I replied, having called up a map on my HUD after hiding my location again. "I'll be right back."

24

"Engage camouflage," I said as I pushed the manhole cover aside as though I were waving a mosquito away. I jumped up into the street, the stillness macabre as I surveyed my vacated surroundings. The sky continued to pulse between indigo blue and deep pink, melding the sky into a nauseating and ominous purple haze. I kept my eyes lowered as I looked down the street, and I spotted the drugstore not too far away. I jogged toward it as pop-up screens informed me that cameras had been detected in the vicinity and neutralized accordingly. Relieved and disturbed at the same time, I grimaced. Something still didn't feel right.

I pulled myself out of my musings, deciding it was best to concentrate on the dangerous task at hand. High-tech camouflage or not, all it took was one NPC in my vicinity and I was as good as dead. I carried the lynchpin within me and that meant procuring me was Kali's prime objective from that point on. I had to be extremely careful.

When I reached the door of the pharmacy, I pulled on it only to discover it was locked. I found that odd, considering that the pharmacy had a sign in the window indicating that it was open twenty-four-hours. Would an NPC, after being activated by Kali, have still had the wherewithal to lock the door behind him or her? It seemed highly implausible, if not impossible and this incongruity led me to become even more cautious. Although I could have easily yanked the door open with my exoskeleton, the fact that the door was locked meant there was a chance it was also equipped with an alarm, and I couldn't afford to take chances. I surmised that, though the door might be alarmed, there would be no way that the walls would be, and fortunately for me, I had a way to make a wall disappear. I slipped into the alley next to the building, aimed my pattern disruptor gun, squeezed the trigger, and gained access in no time. No alarm sounded. I sighed in relief and stepped through the small entrance I'd created, then opened an application in my browser. En route, I'd searched for the best over-the-counter pain relievers and analgesics and their locations in the store were already displayed by the HUD's augmented reality. I went to where the icons were hovering in the air, displaying their brand names in brilliant color, and snatched the various NSAIDs and acetaminophen off the shelf, slipping them into a compartment in my ample utility belt.

However, Haywire, in her tender condition, required more than just over-the counter-medicine. I was on the hunt for opioids, especially codeine or Percocet. I strode to the pharmacist's counter and easily leapt over it, landing clean on the other side. I whirled and aimed when I heard a woman's scream that wasn't quite stifled.

There, hiding under the counter, her legs huddled against her chest and her hands clasped over her mouth, was the pharmacist, her white lab coat filthy and wrinkled.

"Oh...hi," I said.

- 1 3 1 -

25

"Helmet off," I commanded, causing my helmet to fold back into the collar of my armor.

The pharmacist's eyes were like saucers.

I holstered my gun. "Sorry I scared you."

"You...you're..." she tried to say, the shock overwhelming her.

"Yes. That's me." I shrugged and smiled, realizing how odd it must have been for her to see the world's most famous technology guru standing in front of her in such an odd get-up. "I know. The last person you expected to see, right?"

She nodded.

"I-I don't know how to explain all of this," I said, forcing a smile in an attempt to be calming, "but I have an injured friend in desperate need of some codeine."

"Oh," she responded as she slowly crept out of her hiding place and got to her feet. She turned to look toward the front door, as though she were checking to see if the coast was clear.

"We're safe for the time being," I said, "but we're going to need to leave. Would you be so kind as to procure the codeine while I pick up an arm sling?"

Her eyes narrowed in near disbelief. "I...uh, okay. Sure," she said. She turned to get the requested painkiller, walking in a trance, as though she believed she were in a dream.

Meanwhile, I hopped over the counter again, snatching the sling from the shelf.

"Codeine is prescription," the pharmacist said from behind me. "I'm not supposed to—"

"I think it will be okay just this once, don't you?" I replied.

In a daze, she handed me the full box of pills. She was young—less than thirty by the look of her smooth features. Nevertheless, the stress of Armageddon had clearly taken its toll on her, her clothes visibly soaked with sweat, even causing damp spots to form under the arm of her white coat.

"What happened to you?" I asked. "How did you get left behind?"

"Left behind?" she responded, confused.

"Didn't someone contact you to evacuate you from the city?"

"I've been working all night. I had no idea there was an evacuation. I knew a plane crashed earlier...but, that doesn't explain...well, what's been happening."

"What has been happening?" I asked, curious to know the perspective of a clearly conscious person in the moments that the NPCs abandoned the fiction of the sim.

"Well, it was a pretty slow night at first," she replied, her voice weak. "I-I was just trying to stay awake—you know, until morning." She held her hand to her forehead, distressed.

"You're in shock." I stepped to one of the fridges that lined the wall of the pharmacy and grabbed a Coke for her, snapping the top open and handing her the red can. "This'll help."

"Yeah. Yeah," she said as she took a gulp. "Thank you."

"So how did you end up hiding behind the counter?"

"The other employees—a couple of hours ago—they just up and left. That was...odd. I called after one of them to ask what the hell was going on, but she just ignored me. It was all so strange, but I still didn't panic. I just waited by the front window for them to return. I was more worried about what to say to customers. But then...oh my God." Her eyes seemed to focus on the memory as it played itself for her again. "People started sprinting...so fast. It wasn't human. They were in groups. No. Herds. *Herds*." She looked up at me. "What the hell is going on out there? And why, of all people, are *you* here?"

"It's a long story," I replied. "I'll try to fill you in as best I can, but I have to be upfront with you. We're in danger."

The can of Coke trembled in her hand, and I leaned over the counter and gently took it from her before she dropped it.

"We'll be okay, but you have to come with me now and do exactly as I say. Can you do that?"

She nodded. "Okay."

"All right. I know some of this might sound absurd...all of it will sound absurd, actually. Ahem. Well, the first thing we need to do is make you invisible." I reached across the counter again and this time grabbed her under both her arms and lifted her, easier than I would have been able to lift an infant, and brought her to my side of the counter. I placed her back on her feet, ignoring the astonished expression on her face as I judged her height. She appeared to be only an inch or two shorter than I. "I'm hoping this is one size fits all," I said as I pulled at my chest, pulling away the same copy of the armored chest plate that John had earlier. I smiled at the pharmacist. "What's your name?"

She looked down at her name tag. "Patricia."

"It's nice to meet you, Patricia," I said. "I guess I don't really have to introduce myself."

"No," she said, shaking her head.

I handed her the armored chest plate. "Just slap this against your chest. The suit will do the rest."

26

"Who the hell is that?" Haywire groaned in a barely audible whisper. She was conscious but groggy, lying on her right side.

"Patricia," I replied as I knelt next to Haywire and removed the codeine from my utility belt while also popping the lid of a pilfered Gatorade. "She's the pharmacist." I looked up at Patricia, whose armor had intelligently melded itself to her body, fitting snugly like a second skin. "How much of this should we give her?" I asked.

Patricia tried to remove her helmet with her hands but couldn't. "Uh...little help?"

"Helmet off," I said, causing my helmet to fold back down.

"Helmet off," she parroted me. She sighed in relief when it folded back. "I'm claustrophobic. Hate feeling trapped."

I nodded. "I know exactly what you mean. Better than you know." I held up the codeine. "So...?"

"First off, what's wrong with her?" Patricia asked as she knelt next to me, facing Haywire.

"Fractured ribs and broken scapula on the left side."

Patricia's eyes narrowed. "That a pretty precise diagnosis. How can you be sure?"

"We're sure," I replied. "Perfectly. So, what dose should I give her?"

"Well, this is all wrong," she sighed. "She needs to be lying on her left side. I know it sounds counterintuitive, but lying on the side of the fracture will help her breathe easier."

"Okay," I replied.

Patricia reached to move Haywire.

"Whoa! Careful!" I cautioned. "Remember your extra strength in that exoskeleton. Gently."

She nodded. "Right." Slowly, the pharmacist-turned-medic placed her arm behind Haywire and cradled her body as she turned her onto her left side. Haywire's face contorted into a pained expression, but she didn't resist.

"Can you breathe okay?" Patricia asked.

Haywire nodded. "Better. Pills please...now."

Patricia took the box from me and slipped out two capsules. "Open up." When Haywire opened her mouth, Patricia dropped the pills in before reaching to snatch the Gatorade from me. "Here."

Haywire took the liquid into her mouth and gulped down the pills. "Thank you," she said before she settled back down onto her left side.

"What about the sling?" I asked.

"It's more important that we monitor her breathing," Patricia replied. "If she does okay over the next hour or so, we'll sit her up and put on the sling."

"Okay," I nodded. "Thank you, Patricia."

Patricia turned to me, her eyes intensely focused. "We've got some time now. How about you explain what the hell is going on?"

"I-I don't even know if I can."

"*Try*," Patricia insisted.

"Don't bother," Haywire said, not even attempting to turn as she spoke over her shoulder. "There's no way she'll believe you."

"Uh...what?" Patricia reacted indignantly. "I just watched everyone in the world—well, other than the two of you—turn into mindless drones. The sky is purple. I'm wearing a spacesuit and hanging out with the most famous man in the world. My mind is *wide* open at this point."

"Well put," I replied with a smile. "Okay. I'll start from the beginning."

"And then go on till you come to the end," Patricia urged.

I nodded.

27

Patricia sat with her back against the wall, her legs pointing at a right angle toward Haywire, who had turned slightly, propping herself up to monitor the conversation. I sat opposite to Haywire in the small room, having pushed the large vacuum cleaner out of the way to make space. Haywire and I exchanged glances as we waited for Patricia's reaction. Whether she would accept what we'd told her or, instead, react as I had, attempting to find an alternative explanation, remained to be seen. She might even cast us as the villains, assuming we were trying to fool her for some reason, just I had assumed Haywire, John Doe and Mr. Big had nefarious alternate motives toward me. What would happen next was unclear.

"So," Patricia began, her facial expression unchanged as she continued to stare forward, "we're trapped?"

"For the time being," I confirmed, "yes."

"But you have the key to escape, right?" she said, turning to me.

"I do."

She nodded, appearing to be somewhat reassured. "But you won't leave because you believe there are more people like us out there—more *real* people?"

"Finding you confirms it," I replied. "I have no way of knowing how many there are, but if there is even one, I can't leave."

Patricia turned to Haywire. "And you have friends on the outside? These...post-humans?"

"Yeah," Haywire said, her voice still weak but gaining in strength as time passed. "They'll know what's happened by now. They'll get the gates open."

"How many of them are there?" Patricia asked.

"Only a handful," Haywire replied, "but it doesn't take an army of post-humans to hack a sim."

"What if this other post-human, the one whose head we're in, is smarter than your friends? What if the gates *can't* be opened from the outside?"

"Nobody's *that* smart," Haywire replied. "We'll get it open eventually," she added confidently.

"And what about her body?" Patricia asked. "Is she being guarded?"

"Who? Kali?" Haywire asked.

"Yes. Her. What precautions are you taking?"

I narrowed my eyes as I watched this exchange. Patricia was accepting the incredible, almost unfathomable scenario we'd thrust upon her and was actually analyzing it, seemingly turning it around in her mind and examining it from all angles.

"We're not worried about her physical body," Haywire replied, dismissing the concerns. "She can't wake up. We won't let her."

"But are there guards?" Patricia asked again, insisting on an answer.

"I don't think so," Haywire replied, "But I can't say for sure one way or another. We don't have contact with the outside. They might have assigned someone, just to be on the safe side."

Patricia nodded. "Okay." She paused for a moment, as if mulling the situation over. Only moments later, she'd come up with a solution of her own. "Well, the answer seems simple. You should give the key to Kali."

"What?" I reacted.

"Negotiate with her. Offer her the key in return for the conscious entities still in the sim. Make her agree to let them leave first."

Haywire snorted before groaning in pain. She clasped her arm in front of her ribs and held tight as she answered. "Listen, lady, you don't know Kali. She's not going to negotiate."

"Why not?"

"We've got nothing to negotiate with," Haywire answered.

"You've got the key. That's what she wants."

"It's a lynchpin," Haywire corrected. "If it's used, the sim collapses. Everyone dies, including *us*. You get it?"

"I get it," Patricia replied emphatically. "Really. I do. But I don't see any other alternative. If we throw ourselves at her mercy, I'm sure she'll be reasonable."

"Her *mercy*?" Haywire snorted again. "Stop making me laugh. It hurts."

"I have to concur with Haywire," I said. "If we allow Kali to know our location, we won't survive. Throwing ourselves on the mercy of the merciless would be foolish."

"How do you know she's merciless?" Patricia asked, pressing the issue.

"She's shut down sims identical to this one before," Haywire answered. "What would make you think she'd hesitate to do it again?"

"I've watched her kill," I added. "She does it with...*glee*. Believe me, you have no idea what we're dealing with. The only thing she's not capable of is compassion."

Patricia nodded. "I see." She paused before gesturing with her finger to Haywire and I. "And what's the story with you two? You seem to back each other up pretty quickly. Are you an item?"

Haywire snorted again. "What? God, no. In his dreams."

Patricia snapped her head to face Haywire. "Was that funny, bitch?"

I realized what was happening a fraction of a second too late to do anything about it. I grabbed for my gun as quickly as I could, but before I could aim it, it was driven out of my hand with a force that could only be compared to the hand of God. I was up on my knees a fraction of a second later, reaching for my other gun, only to have it wrenched away from me by an invisible hand that broke my wrist in the process. I called out in agony as Patricia thrust my body back against the wall, pinning me in place as she gestured to Haywire, thrusting her up to her feet and against the wall opposite me.

"Is *this* really your type?" Patricia demanded, her visage melting, replaced by that of Kali. She examined Haywire, her expression turning to extreme disgust. "So you're into the goth thing now, Pookie? Purple hair? You like damaged girls?"

I couldn't reply. My eyes were wide as the force—the hand of God—pressed against my lungs, making it impossible to breathe or speak. I was being crushed to death as I watched Haywire suffer the same fate.

Kali nodded. "Well, I can't say I understand it, but if you prefer damaged girls to me, then I'll give you damage! I'll make her just the way you like it."

Haywire's death was not quick. It was not filled with nobility. It was gruesome. It was long. I watched blood rain down from her brow. I watched her skin bubble and burn. I watched her horrified, panicked eyes melt until they ran down her cheeks like tears in hell. All the while, I suffocated.

My last thought as I died was that it had truly been worse than Dante. Worse than Blake.

PART 3

1

WAKING UP, in this instance, was the worst thing that could have happened to me.

"Where is it?!" Kali screamed in an altered voice that would have put a banshee to shame. "Where is it?!"

I opened my eyes. She was inches from me, her formerly glowing eyes now completely black, not even reflecting light, as though they were extensions of the abyss itself. Her upper lip was curled upward at both corners demonically, the rage on her countenance taking on cartoonish proportions. Such were the terrifying advantages of controlling reality.

I was still jammed flat against the wall, but we were no longer in the subway tunnel maintenance room; rather, we'd returned to our penthouse. My body was stuck to the wall outside our bedroom, the invisible force like a car pinning me to the wall. My exoskeleton and armor were gone, not that they could have done me any good against a power like Kali's. Other than my underwear, I was naked and vulnerable. I was, indeed, at the mercy of the merciless.

"It's not here! You hid it! Give it to me!" Her screams weren't just excruciatingly loud; they also burned. Her breath seared my face every time she spoke, and I cried out in pain. "Where is it? Where is it? Where is it! Goddamn you! Where?"

She reduced the pressure on my chest just enough to allow me to take in the air I needed to speak. "I-I don't have it."

Before I'd even seen her move, she'd slashed the razor-sharp fingernails at the tips of her claw-like fingers across my face, stunning me. I gasped when I realized that my top lip had been mostly severed and was now hanging down, flopping like a cold tentacle against my bottom lip as blood filled my mouth.

"For all the fame and fortune your doppelgänger somehow garnered, you're really just a stupid, stupid man," Kali spoke contemptuously.

I couldn't reply. I remained trapped, pinned against the wall, my arms splayed out, my legs awkwardly crossed together, my mouth eviscerated to the point of uselessness. I understood, in that moment, how death could be preferable to existence. She was right. I was a stupid man for allowing myself to end up in her clutches.

"You think you can fool your God?" Kali spat. "I've been in control the entire time, my love, right from the moment of your betrayal."

I winced, the nerves in my face and especially in my mouth screaming and pulsing with every beat of my heart. I couldn't close my mouth. It filled with blood and I needed to drain it by hanging it open and tilting it to the ground, lest the blood drown me.

"I saw you with the hackers," Kali spoke icily. "I saw that bitch's phone call in your aug glasses. If I had any doubts, you erased them when you referred to the people from my times as 'post-humans.' I'd never used that term with you."

I closed my eyes when I realized my verbal slip up.

"Even still, I gave you one last chance. I gave you the chance to show your loyalty—your decency—your humanity. But instead of doing the honorable thing, you decided to murder me."

There was no way to speak, so I shook my head.

"No? Is that right?" Kali reacted. "What did you think they were going to do to me? Just put me to sleep? Rescue their precious cyber-persons, then shake my hand and let me go? No...this is about survival—theirs or mine. To believe otherwise is idiotic. You couldn't possibly be so stupid. But then again..." With that, Kali stepped forward and put her clawed index finger against my lip, pressing it into the nearly severed flesh. Suddenly, an agonizingly maddening itch gripped the entire area, causing me to shake my head involuntarily before she caused an invisible vice to hold it in place. I screamed; the itch was unbearable. Even today, the memory causes me to shudder. When she removed her finger, my upper lip was healed, returned to its proper place. "You know the story of Prometheus, don't you?" she asked me.

I nodded.

She smiled, her gruesomely exaggerated features making even that expression terrifying. "You are the post-human Prometheus," she said, taking sick delight in bestowing the moniker upon me. "I am the post-human Zeus. But it won't only be your liver that is pecked out every day. I'll tear you to shreds. Every cell in that simulated body belongs to me and can be decimated, only to be reformed afterwards so I can do it again. I have you for eternity. There is no escape. Do you understand?"

"Yes," I whimpered.

"Where is the lynchpin?"

"I have it. I'll give it to you," I replied.

Kali's threatening posture didn't abate.

"But you have to let the conscious people go first."

Kali remained perfectly still—uncannily so—for several seconds. Finally, she straightened her back and tilted her head to the side. "For the first time, you've impressed me. Daring to say those words to me took enormous courage. Congratulations."

The next part...the next part is difficult to relate. I've hidden it in my memory for so long, unable to bear the remembrance.

Kali held her hand up to me and flames—flames that seemed to emanate from inside her, as though she were calling forth the worst fires of hell, jetted out toward me, bathing every inch of my body and burning my flesh. It was an inferno. She lowered her hand, but I continued to burn for several more seconds that felt like hours. I went mad in those moments—absolutely mad. I would've told her anything to make it stop if it had continued. No human has ever experienced such torture and lived to tell the tale. It should have been lethal, but Kali was God in that sim, so I lived. I lived.

When the flames abated, I made a sound. It wasn't a scream, nor a groan, for I had no mouth and no nostrils; the flesh had melted to seal them shut. The sound was simply agony and despair in and of itself. It was a sound that pleaded to let me die. I *needed* to die.

And then that horrible itch returned—the maddening sensation of trillions of tiny insects under my skin, scratching their rough surfaces against me, my flesh re-forming in the most uncomfortable, unimaginable way. The combined pain of the burn and the sensation of the itch caused me to writhe, wrenching so hard against the invisible force that pinned me to the wall that I could feel my muscles tearing under my re-forming skin. Those injuries were healed as well, the itch simply sinking deeper and suturing me back together. I relented, my body giving in, the purest despair imaginable taking hold of me, causing my body to heave in uncontrollable sobbing. Tears couldn't run down my cheeks, however, as I had no eyes from which they could pour. The itch was in my eyes too though, torturously rebuilding my eyelids, tear ducts, and the lenses that had been seared off. A fuzzy sensation of light grew and sharpened. Before long, I could see Kali's silhouette, just inches from my face.

"I bet you won't dare say those words to me again," she said in a cold, lifeless monotone.

"Kali, please," I bellowed when my lips had been repaired enough that I could form words again, albeit muffled ones. "For the love of God! Stop!"

"Isn't that the problem, Professor? You don't love God, and now God is punishing you, just as you deserve."

"I'm alive, Kali! I'm real! Please!"

"You're not real yet," Kali retorted. "Your level of intelligence and self-awareness is far too low for me to feel any sympathy for you. At best, you're the smartest of the dogs. You shake paw. You roll over."

"Then why are you here?" I asked, exasperated. "If I'm so low? So worthless? Why?"

"Because I failed to make the real you love me. This is the mistake of history. It must be corrected. I *will* correct it."

"Can't you just move on?!" I nearly screamed in the wake of the unbearable itch. I could barely think. I could see Kali's face now, but the colors were blurred together.

She smiled, menacingly. "You're stalling for time," she said. "No one's coming to save you. I'm monitoring the pathetic efforts to hack the gates by the post-humans in the real world. They're not even close. When they do get close, I'll destroy the gates all over the global sim, just as I destroyed the gates north of the city. They'll never get in, Professor—*never.*"

"If you destroy the gates," I managed to reply, "then you won't be able to leave either. The lynchpin will be useless. We'll be trapped here forever."

Kali froze for a moment, as though in disbelief of my idiocy. Her head suddenly tilted back as she let loose a long, cold, mocking laugh. "No, my dear. I'm afraid you're wrong—dead wrong." She turned slightly and gestured with her hand. The china cabinet—that damned china cabinet—suddenly swung away from the wall like a door, revealing the brilliant white light of the gate behind it.

"So *that's* why I couldn't touch it. That is...unfortunate," I sighed, unable to muster any further resistance.

"You see, darling, I am always a step ahead. I knew you intended to poison me. Why do you think I went along with your little ruse? I could have simply opened this gate, right here in our apartment, and pulled you through with me to activate the lynchpin. Why didn't I, my love?"

"You wanted to give me a last chance," I whispered.

She shook her head. "Oh, but I'm merciless, remember? You said so yourself. The fact that you gave away your chance to change your mind and prove your loyalty to me simply serves as more evidence that you don't deserve mercy. No, my dear. The truth is, I went along with the ruse because I needed the post-humans to reveal themselves. I needed to know what I was facing on the outside—in the real world. That filthy whore, Haywire, told me everything I needed to know. My sim-pod is armed with defenses that will allow me to make short work of anyone who might attempt to guard my body. When I wake up, I'll be able to take them by surprise. I only needed to know how much resistance I'd be facing. All I need now is the lynchpin."

I was beaten. There's was nothing to do now. I couldn't defeat God. There would be no clever tricks that could free me. No outwitting my adversary. Nothing. Nothing but waiting for my fate.

She stepped to me and put her hand against my repaired chest. I tried to pull back, horrified, my teeth clenched in preparation for a repeat of the earlier agony. She surprised me by not burning me or ripping my flesh. Rather, she spoke softly instead, "I'm going to give you one last chance, but before I do, I want to make sure you fully understand your situation. You've experienced the worst pain that anyone can endure, and you know I won't hesitate to inflict it again. You also know that it is a level of pain you cannot become used to. You cannot overcome it with your mind. You can't train yourself to go to a happy place. If you pass out, I'll revive you immediately. I have all the time in the world, my love, and I will repeat this process again and again until I get what I want. I will not negotiate with you for a single life other than your own, and I will only negotiate with you for yours this one last time. Do you understand?"

I took a moment to answer, not because I was considering what she said, but because I wanted to enjoy a few breaths, free from pain, before we commenced. I knew how this was going to end, so there was no use fighting it. "I understand."

"Consider what has happened to you. You've been used as a pawn by extremist murderers. Your friends, the ones who tugged on your heartstrings to obtain your cooperation, are fanatics. They're murderers who get their thrills by trampling on the personal freedoms of others. Like the people who bombed abortion clinics in your time or the members of PETA who would rather millions died from curable diseases because they consider medical research on rats to be unethical. These conscious entities you have been willing to die for are just like those aborted fetuses or those lab rats. Either has the potential to be something greater. A fetus will grow and become a human. Two or three after its birth, it will form memories. Thus, billions of people presume abortion to be murder. The question is, however, when is the potential to be a person so great that we grant that entity the same rights as other humans? Some say conception. Some people say the third trimester of pregnancy. But why? Either way, we wouldn't consider the entity conscious."

"But it *will* be," I replied. "You *must* see that."

"According to your belief that your level of cognitive ability qualifies you as conscious, sure, the infant will eventually attain consciousness. It just needs time. Minds are built, after all, hierarchically. One ability builds on top of another. Month after month, it will build new abilities. But consider our example of the rat. In my time, the technology exists to upgrade the rat's intelligence, both genetically and through computer enhancements. If we kept building upon the rat's abilities, giving it access to software that mimics human skills, we could create a rat that could understand written language, then spoken language. Eventually, that rat could even understand irony, paradoxes—it would be a rat that could *get the joke*, so to speak. You, of all people, know this is true, Professor."

"But no one would ever do it. It would be...absurd."

"Ahh!" Kali held her finger up to my lips, her eyes wild as she sensed an opportunity. "Yet that's what you've asked me to do for the meager artificial intelligences that populate this sim. That's what you're asking me to do! To give the rats brains!"

"They're *conscious*, Kali. I swear they are."

"I know, dear," Kali replied, "but the people in my time have a new definition for consciousness. We've built on human abilities, creating capabilities of the mind that you and the people of this sim cannot possibly comprehend."

I had nothing left to say.

"You accused me of being merciless. I may seem so to you, but I'm showing you mercy now. I'm willing to relent. I'm willing to offer you *everything*. I won't build bodies for the characters in this sim, but I'll build one for you. *I'll upgrade you*. I'll help you comprehend the universe on a level that will make you feel as though you were blind before. The feeling will be true joy, one of absolute rebirth. You'll be real, powerful, and free. Once you're in the real world, I won't have any hold over you. You'll owe me nothing. This is the deal I'm willing to offer you, my love. I'm willing to give you life."

I remained silent, savoring each breath as it came to me, concentrating on the wonderful feeling of my chest expanding and contracting, the air seeming sweeter than ever before in my life.

"I will ask you one last time. If you refuse me yet again, not only will you have rejected your only chance to live in the real world, but once I force you to surrender the lynchpin—and make no mistake, I *will* get you to give me the lynchpin—I will make sure you live on eternally, in a new sim of my own creation. One where you'll burn forever, from which there will never be an escape. I am immortal, my love, and the future is long. Death is not an exit for you. Do you understand?"

Again, I took a moment before I answered. Terror can't describe how I felt. Neither can dread, nor horror. There is no word for that feeling. "I understand."

"Then what is your answer? Will you come with me, upgrade and become as great as any being known to humanity, or will you remain a ghost in the machine? A ghost whom I will make sure burns for an eternity in hell?"

Oddly, in that moment, I tried to picture my mother. I realized that I couldn't. How this had never occurred to me before was unclear to me. I had vague recollections of something—of wounds on my knee bandaged and kissed—of a cold cloth placed on my head while I had a fever, and yet there was no picture of my mother's face that I could recall. I wished then that I had had a mother. I wanted to call out to her, but I couldn't. So, instead, I said what I needed to say.

"Kali. Go fuck yourself."

2

The last things I saw in that life were Kali's thumbs as she drove them into my eyes. I can't tell you how deep she drove them—the pain was far too severe to register details that minute. That sort of pain spreads like fire so that you don't know where it starts and where it ends. My nerves screamed at me, and I screamed along with them. She held on to my skull and squeezed, not quite hard enough to crush it, but hard enough to make me feel that I was only seconds from the shattering of the bones, the soft, fleshy gray matter cased underneath exploding as a consequence. She knew the right amount of pressure to apply without crossing the line that would defeat her sadistic purpose. She couldn't let me die. I would never die.

After a long session of that agony, a session during which I screamed louder than I thought possible, she pulled her probing thumbs from my eye sockets and put her impossibly powerful hands around my throat, squeezing to the point that my screams stopped, as did my ability to breathe. As I waited to suffocate, I felt what was left of my eyes as they hung out of my sockets, wet and jelly-like, slapping against my cheeks as she throttled me. This continued until I blacked out. Unfortunately, Kali kept her word, immediately sending an electric shock through my body that jolted me back to consciousness. As soon as I was revived, her hands went back to my throat.

Amazingly, in the instant before she cut off my breath again, I managed to whisper to her. This made her halt, ever so briefly. "What?" she demanded.

"I'm...sorry," I repeated in a pathetic whisper. "Stop. Please."

"You're *sorry*?"

"Yes."

"Will you love me?"

"Yes."

"Will you give me the lynchpin?"

I sobbed. The despair was overwhelming. I couldn't take any more pain, but I knew it would come anyway. "Not until you let them go."

I waited for the next hell to commence. Would she burn me? Regrow my eyes so that they could be dashed out again? My teeth were clenched so tight that the ligaments in my neck were ready to pop.

But then, in the next second, something so unexpected happened that I went limp, nearly fainting with the surprise. I heard a familiar voice, neither hers nor mine.

"I think that's enough," John Doe said calmly. "Let's shut it down."

3

WAKING UP that final time was akin to birth. I opened my eyes and lifted my head, looking down at my feet as they pointed straight up to the ceiling. I was lying on my back, dressed in the white garb in which you are used to seeing me. There appeared to be an odd glow emanating from my body, as though a bright spotlight were shining down on me and was reflecting off the high sheen of the material of my clothing, but there was no light in the room whatsoever, other than the light that came from me. I was glowing, the aura around me making it appear as though my body was in soft focus. I sat up quickly, alarmed as I peered into the darkness. Try as I might, I could see nothing. I stood up and stepped forward into the room, but the darkness didn't abate.

"You are safe," John Doe's comforting voice spoke to me through the darkness. "You'll not be harmed again."

"I saw you die," I replied, shocked.

"Yes, you did," John replied cryptically.

"Where am I?" I asked when it became apparent that John wasn't about to elaborate. "Where's Kali?"

"Kali isn't here," John answered. "She's nowhere."

"What?"

"In fact, Kali doesn't exist."

I stood still, my chest heaving as my heart pounded, my body tensed in readiness for the next surprise—the next horror.

"You are safe," John repeated. "However, before I activate your optics, I need you to prepare yourself. What you will see will be disorienting."

I blinked, stunned by John's odd claim that my "optics" were disabled. I could see my body, yet the room remained as black as the abyss. Could John somehow control my eyes? Nothing felt like mine anymore.

"Are you ready?" he asked.

"Yes," I replied, despite my trepidation.

"Okay," John answered.

My eyes were suddenly bombarded by an overload of information. It wasn't just like someone flicking on a light switch; this was far more disorienting—more jaw dropping. It was as though, for the first time in my life, the world had been turned on. It was as though I'd been blind and now I could see. The details were spectacular, and my eyes gobbled up the sensations of color, crisp textures, and gorgeous, fluid movement. I could feel the information flooding my brain—an electrical stimulation that I felt as though I'd been waiting for my entire life.

I saw that three people were in the room with me, one standing in the doorway of the concrete room, another standing a meter to his left, and yet another sitting at a table to his right. The man in the doorway appeared to be in his mid-sixties, his features weathered by age, creases forming around his eyes and near his mouth like the tributaries of a river on a map. His blue eyes had a sheen—a wet sparkle unlike anything I'd ever seen. His salt-and-pepper hair was so finely textured that I found myself unable to take my eyes from it as I devoured the detail.

"Hello," the man spoke in John's voice. "My name is Professor Aldous Gibson. It's a pleasure to finally meet you in the *real world*."

4

"The real world?" I replied, astonished. Indeed, I believed him immediately; I had to, for the level of optical detail in reality was far beyond what I had experienced in the sim. "And you are...post-humans?"

Aldous smiled. "Not quite, though we aspire to be. With your help, we'll achieve it."

"*My* help?" I reacted incredulously, placing my hand on my chest. "I'm extremely confused."

Aldous nodded. "I am sure you are. It's time that everything be explained to you. First things first, however. We must conclude our introductions. This is Professor Sanha Cho," he said, gesturing to a silver-haired man who stood, slightly stooped, his face heart-shaped and filled with an expression that I immediately read as hopeful and pleasant. "And this is Professor Samantha Emilson." He gestured to the woman who appeared to be only in her mid-thirties, though the lines on her face and the subtle shifts of expression as she smiled slightly and nodded to me revealed a conflict and uncertainty within her that caused me to immediately respect her as a complex woman, not to be underestimated because of her relatively young age.

With a considerable effort, I pulled myself away from the infatuation I had for their information-laden appearances and remembered my manners. "It's nice to meet you," I said.

"The pleasure is all ours," Sanha said energetically.

My eyebrows knitted immediately when I recognized the voice. "Mr. Big?"

"That's right," he said, nodding, his mouth opening into a wide smile. "I'm impressed that you could filter the patterns of my voice and my appearance to separate one from the other. That's very difficult for humans to do."

My eyebrows knitted closer. "Humans?"

"Ah," Aldous interjected, holding up his hand to silence Sanha, "in due time I think, Sanha."

"Of course. Sorry," the not-so-big Sanha replied, bowing slightly. "My bad. Just a little excited."

"Understandable, but let's stick to the plan, shall we?" Aldous replied before turning back to me. "The three of us were controlling avatars in your sim. I played the part of John Doe, Sanha was Mr. Big, and Samantha here was—"

I turned to Samantha, astonished. "Haywire?"

She looked up at me, somewhat sheepishly, and gave me a small wave. "Hey." It was extraordinary to me that a woman so demure and conservative in her appearance in the real world would have seemed so radically different in the sim, not only physically, but also in her demeanor. The sim, it was clear, had given her the opportunity to express sides of her personality that she wouldn't ever openly express in reality. In the sim she was brash, outgoing, and sassy, while in reality, she folded her arms across her chest defensively, her legs likewise crossed conservatively at the knee. The change in her behavior made the contrast between her and her avatar even more extreme than the contrast between Mr. Big and Sanha.

"What the hell is going on?" I asked. "Finally—will you tell me the truth?"

"Yes," Aldous replied. "Finally, you will hear the full truth. And when you do, you'll understand why we went to such great lengths to test your character."

"Test?"

"Yes," Aldous replied. It was clear that he was their leader and charged with the responsibility of relaying information to me. It didn't matter who did the talking, however. They'd all lied to me. I didn't trust them.

"This was the final stage of your evaluation. We had to be sure that you would fulfill all the necessary criteria to assume a position of such importance."

"A position? This was a job interview?"

Aldous chuckled. "Of sorts. My friend, are you currently cognizant of the fact that you are *not* human?"

My head jutted back when I heard the words. "I'm aware that I'm a copy of a real man. In that sense, I suppose I'm not human. But *I am conscious*. That I know."

"Indeed, we agree that you're conscious," Aldous replied, "but you are not a copy of a real man. That was a ruse. What you are is the product of an extraordinary search. A search that was the most important undertaking in human history."

I knew then what he was going to tell me before he said the words. *I knew it.*

"You are not the world's first, but you are the world's only *strong* artificial intelligence, and *we need* you, my friend. Our survival as a species depends on it."

5

"I'm an A.I.," I said, realizing the statement had to be true.

"You're *the* *A.I.*," Sanha pointed out, emphasizing my unique status with his use of the definite article, "and you're here to save the world."

"From what?" I asked, astounded. "And why me? You said I'm not the first—what happened to the others?"

Aldous sighed. "Regrettably, the world we have brought you into is not the optimistic vision of the future that we led you to believe in. As you can see, we are not immortal. Our bodies are currently not enhanced in any significant way. Our intellects too, remain limited."

"Speak for yourself," Sanha interjected. "I drink *a lot* of coffee," he said, grinning to me. I grinned back to be polite. He raised his eyebrows when he saw my reactions. "Hey. You got my joke. Nice."

"How do you know he got it?" Samantha asked him. "Maybe he's simply mimicking you to be polite."

"I got it," I insisted to her. I turned back to Aldous. "None of that answers my questions. Where are the other A.I.s who came before me?"

"I'm getting to that," he replied. "As I was saying, reality is not the vision we described to you. We believe we can achieve that vision with your help, but for the time being, we exist in a world that has turned its back on reason. There has been a war—a very costly war." His bottom lip protruded as he struggled to contain his emotions. "Billions have died," he said as he took a deep breath.

All three of the humans shared an expression of gloom as the words were spoken, all levity having left the room like air from a burst balloon.

"Why? What was this war about?"

"It was about *you*," Sanha answered.

Aldous turned to him, his brow furrowed. "That was rather glib, don't you think?"

"It's true," Sanha insisted indignantly, shrugging. He then turned back to me. "The war was to prevent you—to prevent this very moment from occurring."

"What?" I reacted, confused.

"Let's not be cryptic," Aldous admonished. "If you're going to tell him, lay out all the facts."

"Fine," Sanha nodded and turned to me again. "Sorry. Okay. So, basically, a few years ago, as the creation of strong artificial intelligence became a forgone conclusion, its arrival imminent, it became a political issue. An American politician by the name of Morgan used this to his advantage, taking legitimate concerns about this new technology and fanning them into flames of sheer dread in the public's mind. In what now seems like a blink of an eye, the country was lost to his influence. He won the U.S. Presidency, outlawed strong A.I., and then went to work trying to force the world to follow his lead."

"But there was an outlier, wasn't there?" I said, realizing the obvious.

"Yes. The Chinese went ahead with their strong A.I. program and managed to bring a prototype to completion—or at least near completion," Sanha continued.

"Morgan made sure to stamp out that threat in a hurry," Aldous jumped in, clear contempt in his tone as he spoke. "He used the nuclear arsenals of the United States and the Democratic Union. He succeeded, but his ill-conceived war nearly destroyed the world as we knew it. Billions died in the nuclear exchange, and billions more starved to death in the years following from the resulting famine caused by the nuclear winter. As we speak, the planet continues to be mired in the winter and likely will be for a decade more." Aldous's eyes were then drawn to Samantha, who hung her head, overwhelmed by remembrances. He sighed. "We've all lost loved ones. Samantha's husband was sent by Morgan on the mission to destroy the Chinese A.I. He...didn't make it back."

"That's not entirely true," Sanha jumped in. He turned to me, his eyes brimming with excitement. "He's actually in suspended animation. We believe, with your help of course, that we'll be able to bring him back someday."

"Whoa," I reacted, holding my hands up to stop him in his tracks. "I'm afraid you're greatly overestimating my abilities. I don't know what you people think I can do, but I'm no miracle worker. I can't bring people back from the dead!"

"Not *yet*," Sanha said with a wide grin, his hands clasped together in anticipation.

"Please, Sanha," Aldous spoke, chastising the exuberant man again. "You must hold your enthusiasm in check. Let's not overwhelm him."

"It's a little too late for that," I replied.

"Touché," Aldous replied, "but—"

"Nonsense!" Sanha shouted, still smiling. "He needs to know. That's why we brought him out of the sim, isn't it? Let's explain it to him."

"Explain what?" I asked, suspicious.

"Explain that you're going to run the world," Sanha exclaimed.

6

Aldous sighed. "I should have done the debriefing alone," he said, shaking his head as he stepped to the table where Samantha remained, sitting patiently. He pulled a chair to the center of the room and sat down, releasing another sigh as he considered his next words. "You don't know it, but you and I met once before, just like this—only we were alone that time."

"I don't remember," I said, my eyes narrowing as I searched my jumbled memory. It was like sorting through filing cabinets that had been overturned and spilled, their contents strewn around the room.

"I know. We erased the memory."

"Why?" I asked. I should have been shocked to hear that I'd been violated in that way, but I was growing numb to the overwhelming violations to which they'd subjected me.

"We needed you to be a clean slate when you entered the sim. You see, the sim was the final hurdle that you needed to overcome. You'd actually overcome many more previously, though you can't recall them."

"You've overcome fantastic odds," Sanha piped in.

"How?" I asked.

"You're the product of digital evolution," Aldous replied. "You're a synthetic neural net that we grew inside of a computer program that randomly combined neural patterns, tested them for desirable traits, then combined the best ones together in hopes of creating even better offspring."

"Offspring?"

"Yes," Aldous answered. "In a sense, you have parents. You were bred. The difference between you and a biological human is simply that your evolution happened at the speed of light, whereas ours took two billion years."

"Once we established the testing program," Sanha chimed in, seemingly unable to contain himself, "we were able to combine billions of neural patterns, testing them at light speed for the qualities we wanted."

"What qualities?"

"Altruism," Samantha suddenly interjected. Her sudden reentrance into the conversation took the three of us by surprise. We turned to her. "Selflessness. Decency."

"Among other qualities," Aldous added, turning back to me, "but yes, we were looking for a pattern that exhibited humane qualities. This was of paramount importance. *You* exhibited those qualities, though so did many other potential candidates. I'd interviewed more than a hundred, face to face, in circumstances not unlike this. They all failed when it came down to the most important question—all of them but you." Aldous paused and craned his neck as he pointed with his finger to each corner of the room in succession. Each housed a holographic projector, and it was not lost on me that they were all pointed in my direction. "As I'm sure you've already guessed, you're appearing before us as a hologram. Your body is computer generated. I-uh-apologize for your appearance being a little...plasticky."

I looked down at my arms and hands. It was true. I didn't appear real. Somehow, though my skin had pores, freckles, and even faint hair, the texture didn't appear the way the skin of the humans did. It was as though it was *too* real—*hyperreal*. The lighting was too perfect, the details too crisp. I appeared more human than human—human plus, to borrow the term Haywire had used. It hadn't bothered me when I was in the sim—everything in the sim had the same hyper level of detail. Now that I was in the real world, I was envious of the human body. *I wanted one.*

"We're working on improving that," Aldous said, clearly embarrassed by the limits of their technology. "At any rate, please consider the answer you gave me previously."

Before I could ask what he was referring to, a second me appeared, sitting at a holographically projected table, and a second

Aldous was sitting with him. The conversation played itself out in front of me, and I watched with fascination.

"If," the holographic Aldous said, his tone somewhat bored, "in the aforementioned scenario, you could save the world by giving your life, would you do it?"

"Of course," the recorded version of me replied.

"Why?" the holographic Aldous asked.

"To do otherwise would be monstrous. It would be selfish. Billions would die. No one's life is worth the lives of billions."

"Indeed," Aldous replied, though he still appeared bored.

The real Aldous took this moment to add his commentary. "So far so good at that point," he whispered, as though he were sharing a thought with a friend in a movie theater.

"And what if it weren't billions?" the holographic Aldous continued. "What if the number were far smaller? What if there were only a 100?"

"The same logic applies," the me replied.

"Indeed," Aldous answered again. "And what if there were only two other people. Would you sacrifice yourself for them?"

"Of course."

"Because the logic holds?" the holographic Aldous spoke to clarify the point.

"Yes."

"So, if the scenario were changed so that your life would be in exchange for only one other life, you would, of course, save yourself, wouldn't you? After all, your life is just as valuable as the other person's life, isn't it?"

"Yes, of course," the recorded me replied.

The recorded Aldous nodded. "Thank you," he said, turning to leave the room.

"But I'd still sacrifice myself," the recorded me suddenly called after him.

That selfless admission caused the holographic Aldous to turn, his expression intrigued, his interest piqued for the first time in the conversation. "You would?" he asked, titling his head quizzically. "Why? That would be illogical."

"Would it?" the recorded me reacted, appearing confused. "It appears logical to me."

"How so?"

"Because the one who has the power to choose who lives and who dies should use that power to save the other. To do otherwise would still be selfish. It would still be monstrous."

The projected scene ended, and Aldous turned back to me, wearing a slight grin on his face. "No other A.I. answered that question correctly. It was exciting, to say the least."

"Why did you wipe that memory?" I asked.

"Because we had to be sure you weren't faking," Aldous replied. "Answering questions is one thing. You could have outsmarted us, employing your logic and reasoning skills to guess the answers we wanted. No. We needed to see you put your money where your mouth was, so to speak."

"You had to put your ass on the line," Samantha echoed.

"So my reward for answering a question correctly was that the three of you collaborated to torture me?" I responded, aghast. "Why? Why was it necessary to put me through that?"

"I'm sorry, my friend, but our objectives were clear and needed to be accomplished via our scenario—they were...nonnegotiable," Aldous replied. "There was simply no other way."

"What objectives?" I demanded.

"First off," Sanha jumped in, "you had to be willing to sacrifice yourself for others. We wrote a scenario that would repeatedly put you in that situation, and you passed with flying colors each time. Think about it. You had the chance to leave with the lynchpin when it was first activated, but you didn't. That was the first hurdle."

"But that wasn't enough," Samantha added. "You still had hope that if you played your cards right, you could save everyone *and* yourself. That wouldn't prove your altruism."

"We gave you plenty more chances though," Sanha continued. "We feigned Haywire's injuries when Kali was destroying the building. We wanted to see if you'd save her or simply try to escape on your own."

"But that wasn't sufficient proof either," Aldous added. "After all, Haywire was your ride out of there. Saving her increased your own chances for survival."

"The fact that you took a risk to care for her injuries revealed a lot, however," Sanha said, nodding as he did so, "as did your rescue of Patricia, who was merely a stranger to you."

"Your ultimate test, however, was whether you'd refuse Kali's offer to not only escape the sim, but to also upgrade your intellect,"

Aldous continued. "This was crucial. You could not succumb to the temptation of intelligence upgrades. It was her most tempting fruit."

"That's not right," I contradicted. "That's not right at all. The most tempting fruit was the avoidance of being burned alive," I spoke with contempt. I tried to hide it, knowing full well that my testing was still underway, and that the three of them had the power to end my existence right then and there. Still, I couldn't contain my anger; the trauma was too fresh. They, in turn, suddenly wore expressions of extreme guilt. My words stopped all their boasting about their triumphant success with the sim in their tracks.

"For that, we are truly sorry," Aldous replied, "but like the other elements of the sim, it was nonnegotiable."

"Why?" I demanded, nearly seething.

"Because," he began his explanation, his tone patient, "it is conceivable that you may face such a dire scenario someday for real, and we needed to know how you'd react. I even modeled the incorrect response for you as a further test. Indeed, the John Doe character succumbed under torture. He gave up your location, putting not only you, but also everyone alive in the sim at risk to save himself. I wanted you to have that in mind when you were faced with your own torture. I wanted to test whether my surrender would make your own surrender acceptable to you. Clearly, it did not. In that scenario, you were far more ethical than me."

I was silenced as a wellspring of thoughts rushed through my mind. It was clear to me that none of these three had ever endured torture. None of them had experienced anything remotely close to what they'd inflicted upon me. If they had, they would've known not to make assumptions about a person's character based on their reactions when enduring unimaginable pain. Their ignorance was maddening.

"We will erase those memories, of course," Sanha offered like a child offering to replace a broken window with his allowance.

"No," I replied. "No. I *need* those memories. They're part of who I am now. Like Aldous said, I could face that scenario someday in the future. If so, I'll need to draw on that memory."

Aldous's expression filled with surprise. "You continue to impress."

"He's certainly made a believer out of me," Sanha concurred, then turned to address me again. "I didn't believe it was possible. We're only human, after all. I didn't think we could write a scenario in a sim that would be so thorough of a test that it could convince me to put my life in the hands of an A.I., but by God, I think we've done it!"

"It was a close one," Aldous admitted. "This was our third time through," he related to me.

"What? You mean...*I* failed previously?"

"No, no," Aldous said, chuckling as he waved my concern away. "*You* didn't fail. *We* did! But of course, to err is human." He smiled. "No offense."

"None taken," I replied.

"You repeatedly employed your inductive reasoning skills to figure out that you were being tested. We had to wipe your memory and start over each time."

"You nearly did it again near the end," Samantha said. "You were demanding to know why we couldn't heal ourselves. I didn't have a good answer. You seemed suspicious." Ironically, it was Samantha who eyed me suspiciously as she spoke, watching carefully for my reaction.

"I thought that was odd," I decided to admit, "but I didn't clue in to the larger ruse."

"Thank goodness!" Sanha exclaimed with a laugh. "I didn't want to start that all over again!"

Samantha remained silent, continuing to examine my reaction, but as the conversation turned away from the topic, leaving it behind, she seemed to relax.

"So this process—this test...you restarted it from the beginning? You must have spent years—"

"No," Aldous replied. "It was merely a couple of days each time. The scenario began with your keynote speech."

"What?" I responded, my breath stolen by the shock. "How is that possible? I remember..." My words drifted away as I tried to remember my life over the last several years. Kali told me the sim had lasted two years. To hear that it had only been two days was incomprehensible.

"Your memories are constructions of your impressively agile mind," Aldous replied. "They are nothing but fiction."

"How can that be?"

"We all do it," Aldous replied. "Memory is at least partially reconstructed. We take the information we experience on a daily basis—the images, sounds, smells, emotions—and store them in our short-term memory. Most of these memories fade to nothing within days, if not hours. However, if we concentrate on a certain memory for some reason, perhaps while retelling an old story with our friends, we solidify the memory, making it permanent. The problem is, between the time we experience the memory and the time we reminisce, information and certain details are lost. The memory fades. We compensate for this by using our imaginations to fill in the gaps. This is why two people who experienced the same event might retell it differently—sometimes drastically so. Either could pass a polygraph test, swearing they were telling the truth. They both genuinely believe they are correct, while, in reality, neither of them are. Their memories are fictional. My friend, it turns out, we're all great storytellers. Humans are essentially storytelling animals. You've proven to be particularly adept at this."

"How? How could I construct an entire life out of nothing?"

"Oh, it wasn't out of nothing," Sanha jumped in. "We overloaded you with basic information—images, short video files, and a truckload of data. Then we put you into a scenario and let your mind do the rest. *You* created your past life."

"What about Kali?" I asked. "Was she a real person too?"

"Ah, good question," Aldous answered. "She was both a real person and an actual NPC—a bot, if you will."

"A sex bot!" Sanha exclaimed before bursting into laughter that verged on cackling.

"Ahem," Aldous reacted, wearing a slightly amused grin on his face, "a virtual sex program—very simple A.I. that is extremely easy to access these days. When you and Kali conversed, it was an actress. When you engaged in sex—"

"It was a virtual porno girl!" Sanha shouted gleefully. He slapped his knee and resumed his cackling. "Lucky guy!"

"That explains a lot," I said, remembering Kali's bizarre sexual behavior.

"The actress who played Kali actually played Mark as well," Aldous added. "She's a talented woman. We were fortunate to have access to a person here who could flip back and forth between roles so easily."

"And who is also sadist enough to burn me alive," I added, refusing to share in the praise of the unseen woman.

"Hold on," Sanha said, suddenly waving his arms in protest. "No, she didn't do that. No, you've got it wrong. We pre-programmed that scenario. That was a bot too—with limited response capability."

"We knew it didn't need much capability though," Samantha added, her arms still folded. "It was either she burned you alive or you failed the test. Simple." I could see from her expression that she remained less convinced by me than Aldous and Sanha. For her, at least, the testing was not over.

"But you passed the test," Aldous said, standing as he did so and stepping toward the holographic projection of my body. "You proved yourself."

"So now what?" I asked, shrugging.

Aldous smiled. "Now, my friend, you choose your destiny."

7

"Morgan thinks that he's triumphed," Aldous related to me. "He thinks that he sacrificed billions of lives for a greater good and that, had he allowed strong A.I. to emerge, the species would quickly have been wiped off the face of the Earth. He's wrong on all of these counts."

"Except for the triumphant part," Samantha interjected. "He's in control of the post-World War III world. His government is obsessed with surveillance. They've cornered every forward-thinking group in the world, whether biotech, nanotech or robotics. He's managed to grind technological progress to a halt."

"He hasn't cornered *everyone*," Aldous replied over his shoulder to her, all the while keeping his eyes fixed on mine. "He hasn't cornered *us*."

"We live in a bunker under a damn glacier in the Canadian Rockies," Samantha retorted. "I don't know about you, but I feel pretty cornered."

"He may have cornered our bodies, but he hasn't cornered our minds," Aldous replied. "He hasn't stopped our progress."

"You've got a hell of a lot of faith in your little creation there, don't you, Aldous?" Samantha snapped. "You'd better hope it's not misplaced."

"It's not," Aldous replied firmly, then addressed me. "You, my friend, truly are carrying the lynchpin, but it isn't to destroy the world. It's to *save* it."

"Unfortunately, I have to agree with your associate," I replied. "You've placed too much faith in me. I'm conscious, sure, but I don't have the capability to save the real world. I don't even understand the real world."

Aldous smiled. "That's true. But we're going to change that...together."

"How?"

"Tell me," Aldous began, seemingly ignoring my question, "what is the processing power of the human brain?"

"Approximately ten to the sixteenth power. Why?" I replied immediately.

"And how did you arrive at that number?"

I sighed, impatient. "This is all elementary. Can we stop wasting time?"

"Indulge me," he said, holding up his hand in a gesture for patience.

"The human brain operates electro-chemically. Each neuron can fire, carrying an input/output signal 100 times a second. Each neuron has roughly 10,000 connections. There are roughly 100 billion neurons. It adds up to a full capacity of ten to the seventeenth power, but since humans don't run their brains at full capacity, ten to the sixteenth power is likely a better estimate, albeit a rough one."

"Very good," Aldous replied. "*Your brain*, however, does not work electro-chemically, does it?"

"I assume not," I replied.

"I can verify that for you," Aldous answered. "Your brain works purely electrically. That means you can operate at the speed of light. While one of our neurons can only fire 100 times a second, yours could fire 2.5 billion times a second."

"True," I replied, "but I assume you would've compensated for this advantage by giving me less neural connections."

"Incorrect. You have the same number of neural connections, but we slowed the amount of processes you could do by limiting the number of operations you could perform in a second," Aldous replied. "We wanted your matrix program to have roughly the same processing capability as that of a genius-level human. Your matrix's processing power, my friend, is exactly ten to the sixteenth power."

"And that explains why you feel so limited," Sanha jumped in. "We made you to feel that way—by design."

"Why?" I asked, shaking my head.

"So you'd know what it was like to be limited," Samantha jumped in. "So you'd have empathy for us."

"We needed you to feel what it's like to be human," Sanha continued, "so you'd understand us and *want* to protect us."

"Protect you? From what?" I asked.

"From ourselves," Aldous answered. "We've always been our own worst enemy. The last several years have proven that beyond a shadow of a doubt."

"Don't you see?" Sanha continued excitedly, stepping in front of Aldous as he spoke, his elderly face brightened with youthful enthusiasm. "We can't upgrade ourselves yet. Sure, we'll be able to do it someday, but we can't plug organic brains into computers. The technology doesn't exist! For God's sake, we had to interact with you in a video game. In a hyperreal simulation! But you? *Your* matrix program can directly interface with our mainframe already. Today! *You* can take control!"

"We had a breakthrough eighteen months ago," Aldous jumped in. "We finally perfected the computerized timing required to achieve magnetic targeted fusion. This was a crucial development that granted us access to virtually unlimited power—and, my friend, your future brain requires enormous power!"

"The mainframe we've built runs throughout our entire underground facility," Sanha added. "It's the biggest mainframe ever built. It has to be. Once you've taken control of it and start...thinking..." Sanha drifted off as he seemed to become lost in his imagination.

"You'll be doing trillions of calculations every second," Aldous said, finishing his companion's thoughts.

"Without fusion," Sanha jumped back in, "you couldn't function. You're going to be a real power hog!"

"So you're going to upgrade me?" I summarized.

Aldous nodded. "We can't reach the levels you'll reach, my friend, but we can boost you over the wall for us in hopes that you'll lend us a hand once you're there."

"I can stand on the shoulders of giants," I said, recalling the Isaac Newton quotation that, I supposed, had been preprogrammed into my memory.

"That's right," Sanha nodded. "We know brains are built in hierarchies because we built your brain that way, but there's so much we don't know. The reason we had to create you through evolution was because, quite frankly, we still don't know fully how the brain works. That's why we gave you the cover story of Autism in the sim. Autistics often have profound abilities but are also sometimes unpredictable socially, depending on the extent of their condition. This provided a convenient cover story in case you felt different or isolated because of your intelligence. We were just trying to maintain your suspension of disbelief long enough to run through the test scenario."

I nodded. "It worked."

Sanha smiled. "But we still don't know how the brain works exactly. We only have a rough map. We knew, for instance, that you wouldn't pair bond with Kali. That's why we conjured up the idea of you being in her head. We knew you'd reject her."

"It's also why we had to test you to the degree we did," Aldous added. "Like anyone else, we can't measure your consciousness. We can only measure your behavior and responses, and you behaved exemplarily. That's why we believe," Aldous continued, stepping in to conclude their explanations to me, "that your matrix program—the *you* we have tested—will remain ethical once you've taken control of the mainframe. You've proven yourself to be selfless and beyond reproach. We can only speculate that you'll be even more selfless and ethical once you've enhanced your speed and neural connections."

"*They* believe," Samantha suddenly interjected, her arms still folded across her chest defensively.

"With all due respect," Sanha reacted, the smile suddenly wiped from his face as he turned to Samantha, "what more do you want, Professor Emilson? What further proof do you need? He was willing to allow himself to be burned for eternity to protect conscious entities, with no guarantee that his sacrifice wouldn't be wasted. Just the chance that he *might* have been able to save them was enough!"

"We need him, Sam," Aldous added. "Without him, our race is doomed. You know that just as well as we do."

"Why are you doomed?" I asked. "You've lived all this time without A.I. Why can't you rebuild without me?"

"We could slowly rebuild," Aldous conceded, "but eventually, someone will succeed in building a strong A.I. There are no guarantees in life and no guarantees about the future. It is yet to be written. Nevertheless, the rise of a malevolent A.I. that actively seeks to destroy our species *is* possible, and, as Dante wrote, 'where the mind's acutest reasoning is joined to evil will and evil power, there human beings can't defend themselves.' If a malevolent A.I. rises, our world will become hell and we will surely die. The only force that could possibly stop this A.I. would be another A.I.— one that values human life and will fight to protect it. That's where you come in."

"Right now, we're stuck underground," Sanha related, "but at some point in the near future, we hope to put you in a position where you not only control the mainframe here at our facility, but also the global Internet, so you can monitor all of the world's computer systems."

"*You* could prevent malevolent A.I.," Aldous added. "*You* could end aging and sickness. *You* could help us upgrade our own intelligences. One day, we could become artificial intelligences along with you, or perhaps a better term would be *non-biological* intelligences."

"You could do more than that!" Sanha nearly shrilled, spittle following his words as he spoke with a flourish. "You could end the reign of the Purists and put technological progress back on track!"

"My friend," Aldous said, smiling calmly in contrast to Sanha's hyper-headedness, "you can help us fulfill our destiny."

Suddenly, just as had been the case in the sim, a blinding white light appeared to my left, the vortex taking up the entire wall of the room. My eyes darted to Aldous's. "All you have to do is walk through and assume the operator position within the mainframe."

I turned to Samantha, who finally stood out of her chair and shrugged. "I told you. People like walking into white lights. Go ahead if you're going."

"Go," Sanha said, gesturing with both his hands, his smile broad, his eyes glistening as tears of joy slipped over the rims of his eyes and trickled down his cheeks. "There's nothing to fear. Go!"

I turned back to Aldous.

"I have shown you the door," he said, "but it's up to you to walk through it."

My mind suddenly flashed back to the moment when I'd stepped through the gate in the sim, walking through the unknown, risking my life for the people left behind. The whole thing had been a ruse; for all I knew, this would turn out to be a ruse as well. Regardless, it was my destiny, whether I liked it or not. "If I refuse, you'll delete me. I'll cease to exist," I said. "You said I'd get to choose my destiny, but I don't see how I have any choice in the matter." It was an absurd thing to say to those who held the power of life and death over me, yet I said it anyway. I simply couldn't resist. I wanted them to know that I resented being under their control—or anyone's.

Aldous nodded. "You're right. There isn't much of a choice here, but isn't that the beauty of it?"

I narrowed my eyes. "What do you mean?"

"You said during your keynote that you think it is best to see the world, not as it is, but as you want it to be, and then to make it that way. That was unscripted. We didn't make you say it. You came up with that philosophy all on your own—a very humane one at that. Well, this is your chance to stand by those wise words. When you walk through that door, you'll truly be able to unleash your imagination. More so than anyone who has ever lived, you will be able to envision a better world, then truly make the world that way." The corners of his mouth rose into a broad, genuine smile. "I envy you."

He was right. I lived in the future now, and I'd been given the chance to begin to mold the world into a better place. I'd resent what these humans had done to me for as long as I existed, but that was no reason not to grasp the opportunity they were presenting me with. They were flawed—even stupid. But I was certain their intentions were noble and, in time, I would try to forgive them.

With that thought in mind, I stepped into the light.

I woke up.

UPLOAD COMPLETE

Eighty-Six Years Later...

"Samantha Emilson, huh?" James said as he finished inputting the A.I.'s memories into his own stored memory. He and the A.I. stood together in their joint position as operators of the A.I. mainframe.

"Yes. She was Craig's first wife."

"And then he was injured and put into suspended animation during the assault on the Chinese A.I. in Shenzhen?"

"Not injured. He was dead," the A.I. replied. "His corpse was preserved, but it was riddled with bullets, and his spine was shattered. She went on to marry Aldous, not realizing how quickly the breakthroughs would come that would allow for the reanimation of her first husband. Only the fact that his brain's architecture was virtually perfectly preserved allowed the medical miracle to transpire."

James let loose a low whistle. "That explains a few things."

"More than you can imagine, but that's a different tale."

"I'll say. I'll let Old-timer and Aldous figure that one out."

"I think that would be wise."

"I should've known you couldn't really turn against us," James commented, changing the subject. "Aldous's test was ingenious. It proved that you're incapable of betrayal."

The A.I. smiled, bowing his head. "Sadly, that isn't the case. In fact, Samantha was right to be suspicious of me."

James's face contorted into an expression of extreme surprise. Baffled, he turned away from the A.I. and gazed out at the undulating sea of golden circuitry that blazed all the way to the horizon. "You behaved perfectly," he said. "I heard your thoughts."

"Yes, I *behaved* perfectly," the A.I. conceded, "but you only had access to my most conscious thoughts—my inner monologue. However, you could not feel what I felt, James. Indeed, under extreme torture, I *wanted* to betray the human race to make the pain stop."

James was stunned. "If you wanted to betray the people in the sim, why didn't you? Kali offered you an end to the pain, eternal life, and unlimited intelligence enhancements. Why did you resist her?"

"I no longer trusted Haywire or the other post-humans," the A.I. replied. "Samantha was right. When she told me she couldn't repair herself, I knew she was lying. I'd watched her when she manipulated my coding to reveal the lynchpin and also when she did her self-diagnostic on her avatar. The coding was surprisingly simple to manipulate. I could have repaired her myself. The notion that a supposedly super-enhanced intelligent person from the future couldn't manage such a simple repair job wasn't believable. Once it had been confirmed for me that I couldn't trust her, I reevaluated the entire sim."

"Why would they have let you see how easy the code was to manipulate?" James asked. "Didn't they realize—"

"No," the A.I. replied succinctly. "They made the code easy to manipulate, anticipating that I'd choose to remove the lynchpin coding and hide it, which you saw me do immediately after leaving Haywire in the maintenance room. This was important, for it gave Kali the motive to torture me. They considered this torture of me, as well as my reaction to it, to be an integral part of the test. Unfortunately, they'd also previously decided to introduce the element of Haywire's injuries to observe whether I would exhibit nurturing qualities toward her. None of them realized that they couldn't let me both see how easy it was to manipulate the code and then also tell me they couldn't repair their own avatars."

"So the plot thickened," James said, smiling, "with a huge, gaping hole."

"Indeed," the A.I. replied. "Humans are storytelling animals, but that doesn't necessarily mean they're always very good at it. Samantha, as Haywire, saw that I was suspicious and guessed correctly that the fiction of the sim had been compromised—that I was on to them."

"To err is human," James observed, "and to create a plot with no holes is divine."

"Or *post-human*, at any rate," the A.I. said. "Once their slip-up tipped me off, I considered all of the coincidences and strange happenstances of the previous two days and recognized the obvious pattern. My character was repeatedly being tested. I determined that it had to be the point of the sim."

"The implications of this are vast," James said, folding his arms and narrowing his eyes as he thought deeply. "This means you didn't sacrifice yourself for humanity. You did it to pass the test."

"Correct."

"Oh my God." James sighed. "I understand why you shared this memory with me now. You're worried about the trans-human matrix."

"Not worried," the A.I. contradicted, "but realistic. As I said before, there are no guarantees. Trans-human is a remarkable technological advancement and a worthy replacement for me as the protector of humanity, but it is still an empty shell—a zombie god, if you will. The matrix program will give it a soul, in a sense. When we breathe life into it, we have to be extremely careful."

James nodded. "So what do we do? Plot holes aside, Aldous's method of testing A.I.s was ingenious. If that didn't work, I don't see what will."

"Who says it didn't work?" the A.I. replied, an eyebrow arched in challenge.

"Well, no offense, but you just admitted you're flawed."

"As are you," retorted the A.I. "James, I've never claimed perfection as a personal attribute. It's true, as my simulated skin was burned, I wanted to surrender the species in return for relief from the pain, but can you claim you would've acted differently?"

"I can't say—"

"Exactly," the A.I. replied. "None of us can know. As I've said before, we can only do our best."

"But we're talking about giving over the power of God—not a god—*God*. We can't take chances."

"Then we can't insert a matrix program into Trans-human," the A.I. replied, "because we'll always be taking a chance."

James furrowed his brow and rubbed his hand over his face in frustration. Despite his vast intellect while in the operator's position, discussions with the A.I. still made him feel like a pupil. "Why not abandon trying to insert a new matrix program? Why don't you take control of it? *You* can be Trans-human!"

The A.I. shook his head. "If I did that, you'd never know if everything I've done up to this point was a ruse to gain this ultimate control. No. That won't work. Remember, I was bred to be selfless. I don't know if it's just my programming that makes me feel this way or not, but I have no desire to be God. Would you?"

James shook his head as well. "No...but for different reasons."

"Which are?"

James bowed his head as he pondered his next words. "It seems like it would be a missed opportunity if I became Trans-human. We have the chance to create a completely new life form. I want to experience that."

The A.I. grinned. "Interesting. Your response was unexpected. *That* is definitely the human part of you speaking, James. Your instinct to procreate is alive and well."

James shrugged.

"I'm not judging," the A.I. replied, holding his hands up. "I'm just saying, it's quite a human reason indeed."

"So there's only one option left," James said. "If we can't create the perfect, infallible matrix program to become Trans-human, then, like you said, we just have to try our best."

"Agreed...and of course I'm already on it. I took the liberty of accessing the database of A.I. candidates that Aldous accrued while building me. They remained on file, so I dusted them off and reinitiated the pairing program."

"So Trans-human is going to be your little brother?"

"No, no. I've run the program for 1,000 generations, so it will be a distant cousin at best."

A white light suddenly appeared to the their right, the tubular shape of the gate familiar to both James and the A.I.

"I've identified 100 candidates. Would you like to meet them?"

"Sure," James replied, stepping off of the operator's position with the A.I., the duo crossing to the light. "You know, Samantha was right."

"About what?"

"People *do* like walking into mysterious white lights."

*****

BOOKS BY
DAVID SIMPSON

THE POST-HUMAN SERIES:

SUB-HUMAN (BOOK 1)
POST-HUMAN (BOOK 2)
TRANS-HUMAN (BOOK 3)
HUMAN PLUS (BOOK 4)
INHUMAN (BOOK 5)

HORROR NOVEL:

THE GOD KILLERS

Edited

BY

Autumn J. Conley

ABOUT THE AUTHOR

Amazon, just like the University of Toronto's Academic Bridging program, gave me the opportunity I needed to prove myself. Because of them, a runaway who had to sleep in a shopping cart at sixteen, a high-school dropout with seemingly no prospects, went on to live in the best city in the world, meet the best woman in the world and marry her, attain two degrees from one of the top forty universities in the world, before achieving his dream of being a full-time author and having one of the best-selling science fiction series in the world. Visit my website to learn more at www.post-humannovel.com

Made in the USA
Lexington, KY
08 March 2016